Delusions of a Side Chick

Delusions of a Side Chick

Kandie Marie

www.urbanbooks.net

Urban Books, LLC
114 Norman Ave.
Amityville, NY 11701

ISBN 13: 978-1-64556-782-0
EBOOK ISBN: 978-1-64556-783-7

First Trade Paperback Printing May 2026
Printed in the United States of America

10 9 8 7 6 5 4 3 2 1

Distributed by Kensington Publishing Corp.
Submit Orders to:
Customer Service
400 Hahn Road
Westminster, MD 21157-4627
Phone: 1-800-733-3000
Fax: 1-800-659-2436

The authorized representative in the EU for product safety and compliance
Is eucomply OU, Parnu mnt 139b-14, Apt 123
Tallinn, Berlin 11317, hello@eucompliancepartner.com

Delusions of a Side Chick

Kandie Marie

CHAPTER ONE

Joe

Things in my life changed after Monica lost our baby 'cause of Eric's stalker. It drove Monica and me apart, so I decided to do a little shopping. I went inside the mall to pick up a gift I ordered a few weeks ago. I went into the store, and when I got to the register, the man at the front brought out the package. He opened the box, and it was perfect. It was just right for her. I paid off my remaining balance, then walked out of the mall.

I was heading to work when I called up my boo, Jalisa. I wanted to let her know how the meeting with Dareen went. Jalisa was so understanding, and her spirit was so free and full of life. I told Jalisa that I wanted to take her out to dinner tonight. She loved it when I made plans for us out of nowhere. I hoped she would enjoy the other surprise I had in store for her tonight.

Later that evening, as I promised her, I picked her up from her apartment a little after seven. She looked gorgeous as she came to the car. She wore this striped pencil skirt with a black blazer buttoned up under her bra. She was showing just enough cleavage, and the skirt hugged her hips and ass perfectly. I was in heaven.

Little did she know this wasn't going to be just a dinner, and I was so nervous. I guess being nervous fucked up my thoughts. We barely had a conversation the whole ride.

We got to Maggiano's in Crabtree Mall. We were seated promptly and ordered two Caesar salads and some drinks. Once the waiter came back with our drinks and salad, he took our order. Still sitting in silence, Jalisa let out an exasperated sound, then went in to find out what my problem was.

"What's up with you?" she asked, taking a sip out of her glass of ice water.

Blowing her off, I kept my head down. "Nothing, ma. Everything is good."

My demeanor was throwing her off. She eyed me up and down. "It is? It's all over you. Did something else happen today that you didn't tell me?"

"No," I mumbled, looking down at my plate.

"Well, what is it? You're barely talking to me. Like, that's not normal." Her eyes got big as she snapped her neck toward me.

"Jalisa, I promise I'm okay. All right?" I slammed my hand on the table.

Snapping back at me, punching her fork hard into her salad, she replied, "All right, fine."

We ate our appetizers in silence. My heart was racing. The whole night, I knew I was off, and it was only because I planned to make a major move. I was a nervous wreck. My palms were sweaty, my heart racing, and I thought of all the what-ifs. I took a big gulp of my Henny and Coke before getting up from the table. I walked over to her, taking deep breaths.

"Jalisa, these past two and a half months have been amazing with you. I have never been in love like this. And the way I love you, the way I feel for you, I don't think I would feel like this with anyone else. I would really love to be your husband. So, what I'm trying to say is, will you marry me?" I kneeled, opening the ring box, nervously anticipating her answer.

She looked dazed when she saw me on one knee, showing her the ring I picked. "You're serious?"

I got off my knee. "Never mind. I know this was a mistake."

"Joe . . ." Jalisa uttered, trying to reach out to me, but my heart and ego were already bruised enough.

"No, I understand. I was a fool." Feeling shamed and like a huge fool, I turned my back on her.

"Joe, yes!" Jalisa screamed, looking deep into my eyes, piercing my soul with those beautiful brown eyes.

"What?" I questioned, my eyes growing bigger with excitement.

"Joe, yes, I'll marry you." She was nodding her head, and her voice cracked as she cried, holding out her hand.

I slid the ring on her finger. "Really?" I was stunned by her response. I wasn't sure what she was going to say, but I just knew it wasn't going to be yes.

"Really, really!" Jalisa jumped into my arms, and I felt nothing but love pour out of her.

I guess I didn't move too fast, and she was just as much in love with me as I was with her. I sat back down across from her, noticing how she just glowed. I was the luckiest man in the world.

"Do you like your ring?" I asked her, hoping it met her standards.

"Babe, this ring is beautiful. But I would've been happy with one from a bubble gum machine as long as it came from you." She leaned over the table to kiss me.

I proposed with a 3-carat diamond ring sitting on a rose gold band, and she loved it. The other couples and workers in the restaurant cheered for us. Jalisa moved over to my side of the table, pulling out her phone to snap a picture of us and her new engagement ring.

My mind was no longer focused on our dinner. I wanted to take my fiancée home. The waiter came back with two glasses of complimentary champagne. I asked him to pack our food to go. After receiving our bags of food, I took Jalisa by the hand and guided her out of the restaurant. When we got in the car, I turned to her, admiring the beauty who agreed to be my wife. We headed back to my home to celebrate, looking forward to the rest of our lives together.

CHAPTER TWO

Dareen & The Private Eye

I woke up a few days later feeling paranoid about the guy who followed me. I wanted to try to find him and see what information could be found about him. So, I retraced my steps to where he started following me. I went back to the school where I first noticed him. When I turned down the street, I saw his car parked out front.

Reneece came outside to meet him. I couldn't hear their conversation, but I noticed him passing her a card or note. Whatever he said, she didn't like it. She got in his face, tossing the paper back at him.

After waiting for both of them to leave, I sped into the parking lot to see what he gave her. The paper was on the ground. Opening my door, I picked it up from the ground and saw it was his business card. He was a private investigator. I flicked the card in my hand before closing my door again. Then I went home and decided I would give him a call.

It was about three p.m. when I called. I was lounging in my apartment, rolling a blunt when I dialed the number on the card, 919-555-5892. The phone rang three times before they picked up.

His voice was so deep, like Barry White, when he answered. "Private Investigator Smith here."

I cleared my throat to change my voice and soften it a bit. “Hi, my name is Monica. I was given your card from a mutual friend. I could use some help.”

“A mutual friend? Who, may I ask?” I could hear him spark his lighter.

“They told me not to say. Everything is really confidential. They were even a little worried you might be upset with them for giving me your information. So, to keep y’all’s relationship intact, I’d rather not say.” I hoped he bought that, ’cause shit, it was hard coming up with something quick.

He chortled, then said, “A’ight. Well, what’s the issue?”

“Well, I wanna make sure you can help me. What do you specialize in?” I was probing him to see if I could figure out why he was with Reneece earlier.

“I can handle anything. Would you rather meet in person to discuss the problem and what you would like done?” the private eye asked me.

“Yeah, that would be awesome. Can we meet later today? Can I send you my address?” I questioned, hoping to lure him into my home and go from there.

He eagerly agreed. “Sure, this is my cell number you called, so just text it to me. What time?”

“Give me about an hour, and I’ll meet you. How much money do I need when you come?” I needed it to sound like I was really about this business transaction.

You need “$5,000 up front unless you need something drastic. All right, Monica. See you then.” He hung up after receiving the address to my apartment complex.

I had an hour to come up with a plan if he came ready for a fight. Always supposed to stay ahead of the game . . . I threw on some shoes, grabbed my keys, and went to my storage locker off Fayetteville Street. Once there, I took some gloves and my 9 mm. If it came down to it, I was going to put up a fight, and we could both die today. When

I got home, I stopped in front of my full-length mirror hanging behind my main door. I looked at myself, wondering if this was the right choice.

"Maybe I should've chosen a public place," I said to myself, tossing my bag of goodies on the floor.

My reflection shook her head. "*For what?*"

"Because he could be with the police. Then what about getting our Eric back?" I asked, rubbing my cheek through the mirror.

Bucking up her chest at me, she said, "*And if he is, we make sure we dead him before he can get back up. Remember who the fuck we are, Dareen!*"

"This may be a mistake." I tossed my head back, then looked back at my reflection. She seemed so disappointed in me.

Bitch slapping myself, I said, "Bitch, get it together. We ain't no pussy. You use that pussy of yours and get him on our side. We can always use an insider to help us stay on top of our game."

I looked around, realizing I needed to hide all my pictures of Eric. In a rampage, I went through, snatching down everything, then carrying all I could to my bedroom closet. I didn't want to show any signs that I was still thinking about him, just in case this private investigator was working with Durham PD. I finally got everything in my closet when I sat on my bedroom windowsill, noticing his car pulling up. I was smoking my Black & Mild when my phone rang.

"Hello," I answered, blowing smoke into my window.

Making his voice deeper than earlier, he said to me, "Yeah, I'm here. Where do I meet you?"

I didn't like the bass in his tone, so I made sure he knew I wasn't feeling it. "Is that how you talk to all the people you're meeting for business? You may want to change that tone."

He got very hostile over the phone. "I'm working on a big case, so if you're wasting my time, I'm out."

I put out my Black & Mild. "Apartment 24-G."

When he hung up the phone, I peeked out my bedroom window, watching a stranger get out of their car. I watched him look around as if he were nervous about coming. I assumed it was the private eye. I popped an Ecstasy pill while waiting for him. I needed to loosen up since I was low on weed. A few moments later, the knock came to my door. When I opened the door, he looked more shocked to see me than I was shocked to see him.

He stepped back from my door, saying, "You?"

Standing in the doorway with one arm stretched to the top, I said, "Excuse me?"

"You were the lady who stopped me that day?" He moved his bomber jacket back revealing his gun.

"Yes, I am her," I said, straightening up my posture and poking my boobs up a little more.

"How did you find me?" he asked, keeping his hand on his gun.

"Please, can you come in? Let's talk inside." I heard footsteps approaching and didn't want anyone in my business that didn't need to be.

We were both curious about each other. Since he now had my location, whoever he was working with would soon know it too if this didn't go well. The PI walked slowly inside, gazing over my body. If this jumpsuit I had on didn't turn him on, he made me want to get in his pants by his stature alone. The private investigator was about five foot eleven with high yellow skin and the prettiest hazel-green eyes I had ever seen. I even got a glimpse of a tattoo on the back of his neck.

Once I closed the door, I turned to get a better look at him. My pussy was purring and ready for some action, but I had business to take care of before I allowed her any pleasure. I invited him to have a seat, but he refused.

"So, again, how did you really find me?" he asked, observing my home.

I wasted no time. I wanted to know what he wanted. "Why were you following me? How did you know to follow me?"

He took my cigar out of the ashtray, holding it in between his index and middle fingers. "I know your name isn't Monica. *I'm* the only one asking questions," he said to me.

I cocked my head to the left side. "How can you be so sure?"

"Dareen, let's cut to the chase. You found me somehow. Just know when you're gone, I'm the one who made it possible, especially now knowing where you stay," he stated, walking through my living room, snooping around.

"Who's to say if this is my place?" If he wanted to play the what-if game, we could too, and I was ready.

"Who's to say I don't call my employer, who's looking for you, and hand your ass over to them? Who's to say there's no one waiting on my signal to come get your ass?" He was enjoying this way too much. The way he was playing with me, he wanted to get me to lose it, and it was working.

"You're bluffing," I said, becoming hysterical.

I started looking through my windows to see if anyone was coming. Then I began pacing the floor. Before I could think of a getaway plan, if that were the case, I took my gun out of the holster under my shirt and cocked it before I turned back to him.

"So, you going to shoot me? You know I'm not just a private investigator; I often work with law enforcement as well. Are you sure you want to shoot me, especially in your apartment? That's not smart. Be smart, ma'am." He taunted, waiting to see if I had it in me to shoot him.

"Stop fucking with me!" I yelled. "Who do you work for? Are you working with the officer who arrested me a year ago?"

"That's for me to know and you to find out." His eyes held mine without any hint of hesitation. I watched him calmly pull out his gun, check the chamber, and take it off safety.

"How can I make sure neither of us finds out?" I asked, lowering the gun temporarily, placing my hand on my hip.

He walked closer to me. "Why are you stalking Eric and Reneece? Especially a year later? Why not move on with your life?"

I had nothing to say. He wouldn't understand shit—no one would. I kept my gun aimed at him. Cocking it, perfecting my aim, I was ready to do whatever to make it out of my apartment.

"If you shoot me, I'm going to shoot you too. So, both of us will die right here. Your choice. Or you can live another day, 'til my boss decides how to handle you." His gun was now pointed at my head. I needed a way to change the trajectory of things.

Licking my lips seductively and placing my gun down near my thigh, I said, "Why don't *you* handle me?"

He turned his head to the side. "What?"

I knew he wanted me. I could tell by the way he watched my ass when I walked. He deserved to know what it would be like fucking with the winning side until I canceled *his* ass. I stood in front of him, releasing my beautiful brown breasts for him.

He kept looking at my body rubbing on his chest. "You don't know what you're doing. This dick will fuck you up."

"Don't I?" I walked over to the rocking chair in the corner.

I removed the pictures of Eric on the wall. I didn't need him snooping around, so I had to distract him. I slipped off my leggings, stretching my legs across the arms of my chair, and started masturbating in front of him. I was enticing him, and it was so simple. His cock was bulging in his black pants.

Removing his shoes and getting more comfortable, he said, "You want this dick, huh? You think it'll keep you safe?"

I sniggered. "For now. I guess. Right now, I want your high yellow ass to fuck me."

"You better say my name too, 'cause I'ma show you what stalking gets you, since you wanna give me that pussy. I'll teach you a lesson you won't forget," he said, all cocky, reaching for his belt buckle.

He stripped down to nothing but his T-shirt and bulletproof vest, releasing his dick. It wasn't super long, but it was thick enough to compensate for the lack of length. I grabbed his dick with both of my hands and slid him inside me.

He backed up quickly and said, "I ain't fucking you without no condom."

"You don't have any?" I asked, standing in the middle of the floor.

He let his defenses down, pressing himself up against me. "No, I was coming to a business meeting, not to get no pussy."

"I may have one in my bedroom. Let's go in there." I beckoned him to follow me.

I heard him engage the safety on his gun and watched him place the weapon on my coffee table as I stood in the doorway. Next, he removed the bulletproof vest and put it on the floor.

I headed to my bedroom, motioning for him to follow me. Before he did, he grabbed his clothes off the floor and went into the bedroom. He set his belongings on the nightstand to his left as I grabbed a condom out of my dresser drawer. Then I stood in front of him, waiting for him to tell me how he wanted it.

"Suck this dick before you put on that condom," he instructed, watching me.

I was stroking his dick in my hands. "You want me to suck it?"

"Bitch," he said as he forced his dick down my throat.

I was sucking him off while he played with my pussy. Then his hands gripped my hair as he thrust back and forth. I opened my mouth wide so his dick could hit the back of my throat. His stupid ass was loving every moment. I'm sure he was having some crazy thoughts. But I planned to pussy whoop him during this session. That way, I can have him on my team.

Snatching his dick out of my mouth, he told me to put the condom on it. I obliged, trying to make sure I gave this nigga the best nut he ever had in his life. His dick was throbbing in my hands. I could feel the veins poking out like they were ready to bust. I slid the condom on his dick, and then he manhandled me, bending me over, arching my back the way he wanted.

He hit me hard from the back, forcefully pumping his eight inches into me. We dirty-talked each other, which turned us on even more. He yanked my hair back, calling me his nasty and crazy bitch. I was loving it. He fucked me that way for the longest.

As we both climaxed, he allowed me to get another nut off before pulling out of me, snatching off the condom. He told me to open up as I kneeled on the bed in front of him. He jacked his dick, getting his nut ready. Then finally I opened up to catch his seeds in my mouth. I swallowed it, but it was super salty. After swallowing that, I needed to smoke something to get that taste out of my mouth.

I took a Black & Mild out of my nightstand drawer. "So, will I see you again?"

He gave me a light. "What you mean?"

"Will I see you again to, you know, fuck?" I asked him, sitting up on the edge of my bed.

He stood up and began getting dressed when he said to me, "It was good, I give your ass that, but I'm being paid to do a job. You safe for now. Before I give you up, I'll let you know. Maybe I'll hit it one more time before my boss does whatever he plans to do with you."

I was baffled. I thought I snatched his soul. Shit, I *know* I did. He was louder than I was. But it wasn't enough to get him to tell Eric to give up. I had to find a way to get him on my side. I needed more time to get my plan together. I wanted no flaws with this shit.

"This won't be the last time you see us. I will see you very soon. Very, very soon," I said, getting off the floor and heading into the bathroom to clean myself up. "You can see yourself out. I have money to make."

I threw him a rag, closing my bathroom door behind me. I waited to hear the front door close before coming back out. He had no clue he was going to be my next victim once I got what I needed from him. I got myself together and left to go meet up with Tommy.

CHAPTER THREE

Tommy

It was a beautiful Saturday morning, and I woke up to the love of my life lying beside me. It's the best feeling in the world. I wanted her to move in with me, especially with our baby. I wanted us to be a true family. But deep down, I was still puzzled about her secretive nature. I was in the kitchen making breakfast, mixing up the pancake batter, when she came in. I puckered up my lips.

"Hey, beautiful, good morning," I said to her after giving her a little peck.

"Hey, Tommy," she said with a smile and kissed me.

"I'm gonna be done with breakfast soon. Just relax, baby. I got this." I turned around, heading back to the stove.

I finished cooking breakfast and fixed our plates. We ate while watching *Law and Order* reruns. Our day was simple and relaxed. We lounged around the house all day. It wasn't until late that afternoon that things went left. We were watching *Twilight Breaking Dawn*, Part 2. Just seeing them together, I know it's fictional, but it just made me want to be deep inside her thoughts. As the movie ended, I thought it was the right time to talk and open up.

I was reaching for the remote when I said, "Monica, babe, you aren't going to sleep on me?"

"No, I'm not, nigga. What are we watching next?" she asked, stretching her arms.

I passed her the remote, then took her hands in mine. "Before we watch something else, I wanted to ask why you're acting so funny every time I ask you about your past, your family, or anything about you in general. Shit, I don't even know where you work. It's almost as if you don't want me to know who you are. Why?" I probed, hoping she would just tell me, but I should've known it wasn't going to be that easy.

"I don't want to talk about this right now." Monica ignored my questions, flipping through the on-demand movies until she found one she had never seen before.

"Monica, babe, we need to talk about things." Keeping my tone warm and inviting, I hoped she would just let her guard down and talk to me.

"Gotdamn it, Tommy, just drop it once and for all, OK? Damn." She raised her voice at me like she was scolding a child, making me sit back.

I wanted her to know that she found everything in a man that she was looking for. The most prominent figure in her life right now, and hopefully the rest of her life outside of our seed would be me. The truth was, I was in love with this woman, and I wanted to tell the world about it. She, on the other hand, wouldn't let me in. It's like she's hiding me, our relationship, or maybe things about herself. But I didn't care. The more I tried to talk, the more she dodged the conversation.

"Tommy, baby, let's just talk about something else." Monica got up and went into the kitchen.

"Like what? Baby names or something?" I asked with a chuckle behind it.

Monica came out of the kitchen with a glass of apple juice. Before she sat down, she took my hands, placing one between her thighs and the other on her pregnant belly.

"I can't wait to see and find out what we're having." I was overly excited at that moment; I even had a list of names picked out.

"Is that right?" Monica tilted her head back to look at me.

"Yeah. Maybe it will be a little girl. Daddy's princess. She'll be as beautiful as her mother." Ecstatically, I clung to her, just thinking about what our future held.

"Yeah, maybe," she smirked before redirecting her attention back to *Law and Order*.

I was sitting there with her, rubbing her belly, whispering to the baby. I loved the thought of having a child, having a family. Monica was dozing off on me when I received a picture message from Eric.

"Monica, babe, look, check this out." I was excited to share the news with her, hoping it would spark some type of light in her.

"What is it?" she asked me, still focused on the show.

"Look, my homie just sent me this." I put my phone in front of her and showed her the picture.

I grabbed Monica from behind, pulling her closer to me. It was a picture of Eric, Reneece, Hailey, Jalisa, and her new man. They were at a cookout Eric was throwing at their home, and I missed it because Monica didn't want to celebrate Jalisa's recent engagement. I wanted her to see the family our child would have, and the friends she could have if she'd just met them. She never asked who they were. She sat there with her head turned as if she was disgusted.

"Babe, you all right?" I asked, noticing how quiet she was.

Monica was sitting there like she was zoned out. "Yeah, I'm good."

"You sure?" I asked, rubbing my hands through her burgundy-colored weave.

She sat on the chair, looking away. "Yeah."

"Just think, one day, this will be us," I said, cheerfully placing my hand on her stomach.

I watched her demeanor change after showing her those pictures. So, I took her by the hand. I had a surprise for her. I had been working on a nursery for our baby, and it was almost complete. I opened the bedroom door to it, but her response wasn't what I was expecting.

"Tommy, I think we need some time apart, " she mumbled as she walked around the nursery.

I was taken aback by what I heard. "What you mean? You wanna break up or something? What are you saying to me?"

"Like what you want, I don't know if that's what I want right now. This is all happening too fast." Monica held the white baby blanket that I had draped over the crib, then tossed it down.

I shook my head with complete incredulity. "Monica, are you serious? Moving too fast? You're not ready?"

She hung her head and walked out of the nursery, saying only, "Tommy . . ."

"Nah, man. The only fuckin' thing I ever asked of your ass is to be real with me. Let me be the man to you that thousands of women are begging to have. I just want you to let me in, but you keep pushing me away. Still, here I am. Shit, I fuckin' love you and our child, " I screamed at her, slamming the door of the nursery behind me.

"*Tommy, calm down,* " she yelled as she walked toward the room.

Following her into the bedroom, I said, "Monica, I just want you to let me in, let me meet your family, and tell me more about you. Like, you know everything about me. Why are you so secretive? I don't want to just be in your pussy. I want to be in your heart too."

"I'm not ready." She turned her head away from me so she wouldn't look at me.

I felt like I was losing her and myself at this point. I never knew loving someone could hurt like this. I just couldn't fathom a real heartbreak or not having her in my life.

Yanking my hand away from her, I said, "Monica, you haven't been ready for damn near six months now." I was growing aggravated with her by the second.

"Tommy, you don't understand," she said solemnly.

"I would—*if* you let me. Damn, how hard is that for you to get?" My eyes were welling up with tears. It was like she didn't want me to love her.

Turning her back to me, she said, "Just fuck it!"

I called out to her as she walked out of my bedroom, "Monica! Monicaaaa!"

"No, Tommy. I just need to calm down. I'll be back later." Monica grabbed a set of my car keys out of the bowl by my front door.

I blocked her from the front door, trying to take my keys back. She laughed in my face, bruising me even more. I asked her nicely to give me my keys as she dangled them in front of me. At this point, I was more than irritated with her.

"Nah, you heard me. If you want to leave, then fuckin' leave. But you're *not* going in my shit," I said, snatching my keys out of her hand. "I've been nothing but good to you, let you meet my brothers, my mother, and told you everything about me and my life. But you start this shit *every* time I try to get close to you."

Monica tried to console me. "Tommy, come on. You're overreacting."

"Nah, miss me. I'm good, ma. Have a nice day. I'll call you later. *I* need some time." I walked toward the garage.

Monica followed behind me, yelling, "Tommy . . . Tommy, you can't do this to me. What about *me*? What about our baby? Huh?" She started hitting me in the back.

I gently pushed her off me so I didn't hurt her. "No. I love you. But you don't love me, do you?"

She stood there, not answering my question. I opened the door to the garage, but she wouldn't leave. I guess she thought I was playing with her. I went to slam the door, but she pushed it back open. One of her bags was by the door. It was as if she preplanned her departure.

"Here, take yo' shit too. You want to leave? It's too soon, right? You need time? Well, take your shit with you when you go!" I screamed at her while throwing her things toward her.

She stood there in shock. I yelled at her again, telling her to get out. Monica said nothing to me. She just grabbed what she could, running out my door. I didn't really want her to leave, especially upset. I was crying, hurt, and confused. I guess that's where the anger came from. I loved her, but maybe she didn't love me. When I called her name, she didn't answer. I dried my eyes, trying to run after her, but she was already gone. How did I let her leave like this?

CHAPTER FOUR

Dawson Smith

The Private Eye

It's been a couple of weeks since I had my first encounter with crazy Dareen. I had a job to do, but with her, I was mixing business with pleasure. We would meet up before my scheduled meetings with Eric or any client I had. Man, shorty was so wild in bed. I loved every moment of the wild sex. My girlfriend never wanted to have sex as much or as roughly. I decided just to play the game. I wanted to know if she was truly as crazy as Eric said, or if he was trying to get rid of his side piece in a fucked-up manner.

I was sitting in the car smoking a Newport when Dareen texted me. I was on my way to have a lunch meeting with Eric.

Dareen: Hey, you.

Me: Hey, what's up, sexy?

Dareen: lol. You must want some more of this pussy.

Me: You want this big dick?

Dareen: Mmm-hmm, why don't we both get what we want?

Me: Send me something to convince me to come over.

Dareen: You need convincing now? Or your little girlfriend gave you some better pussy than I do?

Me: How you know about my girl?

Dareen: I saw her picture and contact name pop up one day when you were taking a shower. Idgaf about her, or what you y'all got going on. Give me the dick.

Me: Look, my girl got nothing to do with what we have. Never speak about her again.

Dareen: Lol. Shit, calm down, nigga. I'll be home around four. Come by and show me how angry you are.

Me: Yeah, I'ma shut yo' ass up with this dick. Leave the key under the mat for me.

Dareen: Oh, I'm pregnant.

Me: Pregnant? We ain't been fucking that long for you to be pregnant. At least, not by me.

Dareen: Let's talk about it later.

I was meeting Eric at the Waffle House. I really had nothing to tell him, but I had to come up with something. The man was paying me $75,000. I had to deliver something. We arrived at the spot within a few minutes of each other. My palms were sweaty as I sat down. I was barely making eye contact.

The waitress, a short, chocolate thang, came up to the table. She had bottom gold grills, purple and black hair, and a few acne bumps on her face, but she was still a little cutie.

Flashing her grill at us, she said, "Hey, fellas, may I take your order?"

Looking down at the menu, Eric said, "Can I get a T-bone steak and three scrambled eggs with cheese and wheat toast? And let me get a Coke to drink, light ice."

She nodded her head at Eric, jotting down his order, then turned to me. "And you, sir? What can I get you?"

I was going to say to her I wanted to have her on my dick, but I was already doing too much with Dareen. I needed to get my dick under control. I looked at her with a smirk and said, "Can I get, umm, two waffles, two eggs fried, and three sausages?"

When I looked back up, she locked eyes with me, and my dick was rising. All I could do was think about tearing her short ass out of the frame. Once she walked away, Eric stared at me.

"Damn, man, may as well get her number," he joked with me. "Now, since I finally got some of your time, tell me what you've found out."

I cleared my throat. "As of right now, I have minimal information. The hospital was a dead end. I found out she had two other sisters. She was one out of a set of triplets."

The waitress returned with our drinks and said our food would be ready soon. We thanked her and returned to our conversation.

"So, you mean to tell me there are two other psychos like her walking around? Have you found them? Are they hiding her?" Eric asked.

Before I could respond, the waitress brought our food to the table. I started digging into mine.

"I don't know yet. I'm still trying to get more information. I'm a one-man army, you know, so I'm doing the most I can at a decent speed." I took a sip of coffee.

Eric got upset, banged his fist on the table, then, under his breath, he said to me, "Listen, here, boy. I pay you enough money to have more than that to tell me."

"I ain't your boy, and I'm going to get it done. You paid me to do my job, and you have to trust me to do so," I responded, gritting my teeth.

"You don't know what she's done to me and my family. So, just get it done." Eric put a hundred dollars on the table. "I need to get back to work. I hope to hear from you with more information soon, my brother. I want to get her before she tries to get us."

Eric walked away with his food halfway eaten. I was sitting there wondering if everything he said was true. The waitress came back to the table, and my dick was talking to me.

"Hey, you good over here?" she asked, taking my empty plate off the table.

"Yeah, I need a few to-go boxes. My business partner had to leave for a meeting." I grabbed a napkin to wipe my mouth.

"No problem. I'll be right back." She walked away, swishing her hips.

That was the first time I caught a glimpse of her rear end. That ass was super phat. All I could think of was how it would look on my dick.

She came back to the table with the containers, and I decided to make my move.

"Hey, hun, here's for the food and keep the change." I flashed a dashing smile at her.

"Thanks. This is awesome. I appreciate it." She happily accepted the money.

"Hey, what's your name? You getting off soon?" I asked her while my eyes roamed over that pretty, petite body.

Licking her glossy lips slowly, she replied, "I'm getting off as soon as I ring you up. Y'all were my last table. What's up?"

"You drive?" I asked, trying to see where I needed to be.

"Nah, I catch the bus or try to get a ride," she said, standing there, poking out her breasts.

"I can take you home. I'm going to be outside in the black Charger on red rims." I winked at her, grabbed my containers, and walked outside.

A few moments later, she came out and met me. I told her to hop in. She said she stayed in Campus Crossing. Those were student apartments for the students at Central, Duke, and the Art Institute. As we were riding, she unbuttoned her shirt, revealing the top of her round, juicy breasts.

She told me to park at building 500. She was about to get out when she asked me to come inside. Without hesitation, I followed her to the apartment. Once inside, we went straight back. I gathered she had roommates from the two other closed doors.

"You want anything to help you feel comfortable?" she asked, taking off her shoes at her dresser.

"Undress for me. Let me see you outside that uniform," I instructed, sitting on her bed.

I watched her turn on some music. Then she slowly undressed in front of me, lazily winding her body to the beat. When she was completely naked, she walked over to me, sitting on my lap.

"Someone is ready," she giggled, while running her hand under my shirt.

As I tossed her on the bed, I said, "Yeah, let me show you." Spreading her legs wide open, I shoved my face in her hidden forest.

Either she doesn't get no dick, or she didn't believe in shaving. Her pussy was covered like a wild forest, but I was going to drink from the water anyway. However, her pussy was a little tangy, and it was throwing me off.

"Please fuck me," she whispered, lying on the bed, rubbing her thighs together.

"Fuck it," I said, reaching into my pocket for a condom.

I slipped the condom on, then pulled her body to the edge of the bed. Sliding inside of her slowly, I felt her pussy tightly grip my dick. She gasped, feeling all this dick inside of her. I dug deep into her pussy, giving slow, deep strokes.

"You gonna take this dick. Don't you put no scratches on me," I moaned out as her wetness covered me.

"Yes, I want it all," she uttered, grabbing the sheets.

"Yeah, that's what you gonna get." I smacked her ass before flipping her around.

I wanted all that ass to bounce on my dick. As soon as I started knocking it hard from the back, shit didn't smell right, making my dick soft-ass shit. I quickly pulled out of her pussy. She needed to douche or something.

"Hey, what's wrong?" she asked, looking back at me.

"Nothin'. I didn't realize the time. My boss is gonna kill me. I gotta run, shawty," I lied. I just wasn't one of those disrespectful types of dudes.

"Well, I'm still horny, and I wanna nut." She sat up on the bed, throwing a tantrum.

She tried to pull me back, spreading her legs wide. I almost threw up the way she smelled. It was like she had a sea of dead fish in her pussy. As cute as she looked and all that ass, it was a fucking waste. But I had to go. Shorty needed to take care of that. I asked her for her number, telling her I would call when I finished working. Then I ran out of that apartment so fast, you would've thought I was being chased.

I got back into my car, heading toward Dareen's place. I couldn't believe what just happened to me. Never have I ever experienced pussy like that. As I drove toward my next destination, I stopped at a gas station to grab some mouthwash. I felt like I could still taste the fishiness on my breath.

I got to Dareen's place and noticed the car she drove wasn't there yet. I knew she had left the key under the mat for me. I got out of the car and headed inside. It was quiet inside her building. I grabbed the key and entered.

This was my first time alone in her place. So, since I had some time, I decided to look around. Her home seemed normal . . . until I noticed a bunch of papers stuffed in a corner behind her nightstand. Most of the documents were just directions, job applications from department stores, but underneath all of that was a folder.

Inside the folder was a year's worth of her observations of Reneece, Eric, and Hailey. She knew their schedules as if they were her own. I took the folder and placed it into a plastic bag I saw on the floor. As I continued digging in that same area, I began seeing pictures she had taken of Eric and had them printed out. Some were pictures of Reneece with her face cut out and Dareen's face replacing hers. Or Reneece's picture was stabbed or burned. All pictures of their daughter remained untouched. Some had little notes beside them, and one said, "*I'll be your new mommy soon.*"

I was disturbed and realized Eric wasn't just making up all those things that he had told me. Shorty was really crazy. I've been fucking up. I took everything I could find to use as evidence. If I ever had kids, I wouldn't want any psycho-ass bitch trying to hurt my family. I decided to keep the evidence. I didn't want Eric to kill her, but I don't want her hurting his family. I had to figure out the best way to help both of them. Before leaving her apartment, I left her a note in the journal she had lying on her nightstand.

I did want to see you tonight, but the more we fuck, the more I'm getting attached to you. I want to keep you safe, but part of me feels like you're using me. I'm done with this, and I'm done fucking you. You call me if there is a baby and tell me when I can take a DNA test. You right if you are asking if I think you're a ho. You may be, 'cause I don't know you. Dareen, wherever your journey ends up taking you, I hope you find peace and become a better woman than you are today.

I tore the page from her journal and left it on her kitchen counter. I also took a picture of it just in case she pretended not to find it. I realized at some point that I would need to come clean to Eric, but when was the proper time? I hoped that Dareen would eventually move on with life, and if she was really pregnant, even if it was only a slight possibility that it was mine, I wanted to be there.

I took the bag and anything else I thought was important, left the key inside the apartment, and ran out to my car. As I swerved out of the parking lot, Dareen was pulling in. I wanted to turn around and hear her side, but I knew she would just lie. I mashed the gas and kept going. I was done with Dareen.

CHAPTER FIVE

Dareen & Joe

I had come home the other day, hoping to find Dawson there, ready to give me some more of that good-ass dick he got hidden in those pants, but instead, I found this bullshit-ass note. How could he do this to me? I knew he was close to being on my team, and for some reason, he tossed me aside like yesterday's garbage.

I wondered if he had seen something in my apartment while he was there, 'cause my door was unlocked when I got home. But I couldn't worry about him too much. I still had bigger fish to fry.

A few days later, I lay in my bed wondering why Tommy had yet to call me. I knew he couldn't have been that mad. I turned over on my side, grabbed my phone off the charger, and called Joe, but got no answer. I lay on my back, placing my hand on my belly.

"I don't want you. I only want a child from Eric," I whispered to my unborn child.

I tried to call Tommy several times, but he ignored every call. As I lay there wondering what I should do, I decided it was time to get rid of this bastard child. How could Eric love me if I got pregnant by someone other than him? I went into my closet and grabbed $800 from my getaway money. I remembered an abortion clinic in Raleigh.

I was able to get the pill. They advised me that I would be in a lot of pain for a few days. I didn't care. I was just happy to get this demon out of me. After sitting in the parking lot of the abortion clinic, I sent a text to Joe about the abortion.

ME: Joe, Joe, please call me back. I've lost the baby.

Joe never texted me back. I was sitting in my car, about to text Tommy with the news, but I figured he should get it in person. I sped off from the clinic in the direction of Tommy's home. As I was approaching, the sun was starting to set. The lights were on inside his home. Parking in his driveway, I prepped my performance. It needed to be perfect, dramatic, but not over-the-top. I got out of the car, feeling the pain starting to kick in. I knocked at the door several times, but no one answered.

"Tommy!" I screamed when the door didn't open. "Tommy, please, open the door."

Finally, I could hear someone approaching. My heart was beating fast, hoping he was by himself, so I banged on the door again, constantly yelling for him. But he took his sweet time to answer me.

"Yeah?" Tommy said, cracking his door open just enough to hear whatever I wanted to say.

"Babe," I said, forcing tears to come out. I tried to open the door wider to grab ahold of him, but he wasn't letting me in.

"Monica, if that's even your name at this point, I'm not in the mood to be arguing over bullshit and hearing all your excuses." He was about to shut the door on me.

"Tommy, look at me, please. I lost the baby today." I held my stomach and gave him puppy-dog eyes.

"What?" he said, slowly opening the door.

"I lost the baby," I blurted out, forcing out a cry. I thought I would have his sympathy, and it would play well in my favor.

Pulling me inside to console me, he said, "Listen, I was being an asshole. I want you to know that I'm yours, and I'm with you. I love you, Monica."

I looked up at him with a smile. I had him. He said everything I needed to hear. If anything were to happen, I knew then that he would protect me at all costs. He fell for my fake cry so easily; it was like taking candy from a baby.

Joe

I was heading to pick up Jalisa from work when Dareen kept calling me. I didn't understand why she kept calling. She needed to catch the hint. Once I got close to Jalisa's job, I turned my phone to vibrate. She got into the car in her scrubs, looking so beautiful. Welcoming her into the car, we kissed before I pulled off. Since we were moving into a new place together, we decided to do some shopping at Walmart to pick up a few things. Starting over, especially with her, was the best decision I ever made.

"So, I was thinking that maybe we should all meet. Be adults about everything," Jalisa said as we walked through the curtain aisle, moving around in the store.

"Who? Who should meet up?" I questioned, unsure where Jalisa was taking the conversation.

"Her. Us. I think it would be best. I mean, we must be in each other's lives together. I'm going to be your child's stepmother, and they will have a half brother or sister," she went on while pulling down a powder-blue comforter set.

"Yeah, hopefully, someday. Maybe someday soon if you keep putting it on me as you do," I declared, cackling.

"Well . . ." Jalisa paused in midconversation, digging through her purse. She turned around, pulling something out of her purse. Standing in the middle of the towel aisle in Walmart, I screamed in joy as I looked at the positive pregnancy test Jalisa handed me.

"You fuckin' kidding me, yo?" I shouted, my heart racing, my spirit was overjoyed.

Laughing at my reaction, she said, "No, babe, I'm not joking. We're going to have a baby."

"Seriously, this is real?" I stopped in the middle of the floor, pleasantly shocked.

She smiled at me. "Yeah, daddy."

In the middle of Walmart, I grabbed her, spinning around with her in the air. I was so ecstatic to hear that my soon-to-be wife was having our baby. I couldn't be happier.

"Well then, we definitely need to have a family meeting now," I suggested. "I know our parents have been wanting to meet, especially since the engagement."

"Yes, our mothers are going to be ecstatic. My mom been asking about a grandbaby for a while now." I continued to push the cart around the store, shaking my head.

"Well, my mom already loves you more than she loves me. She talks about you all the time," I expressed to her while letting out a light chuckle.

"Did she ever meet your ex?" Jalisa asked, sounding very curious.

I shook my head, following behind her. "Nope. She only knew I was messing around with some girl named Dareen. I tried to make an honest woman out of her, but she was too busy doing her own thing and fuckin' whoever."

Jalisa pulled me close and said, "Well, you got me now and forever."

We shared a kiss in the aisle before continuing to shop. While walking through the baby section, I glanced down at my phone, noticing a text Dareen sent me a few hours ago. I read it several times and couldn't swallow it.

I slumped over one of the fixtures, trying to fathom what was happening. Jalisa came up to me, asking what was wrong. I pulled myself together, kissed my fiancée on the cheek, and whispered that I was okay. She just wrapped her arms around me. This was a bittersweet day. I hoped Dareen wasn't playing a sick game, but if it were true, I was partially relieved because I was completely done with her for good now.

CHAPTER SIX

Reneece & Eric

Jalisa and I were out at Northgate Mall just having some much-needed girl time. I hadn't been able to catch her up on all the craziness about Dareen. She had a right to know. She could come after any of us, and we needed to be prepared. I know she felt that I wasn't supportive of her engagement to Joe, but I just wanted to make sure my girl was happy and with a real man. We made our first stop inside Sears after grabbing a fresh Cinnabon from the middle of the mall.

Jalisa stopped at the front entrance near the children's area, spotting a cute unisex onesie folded on a display table.

"Isn't this cute?" she asked with a glow, holding it up to show me.

"Yeah, it is. Since when were you so excited to be a stepmom? Did you meet the baby momma yet?" She was so giddy that it made me a bit suspicious.

"Nah, still haven't met her. But I'm not going to be a stepmother anymore. I'm just going to be a mother," she replied, placing the onesie over her left arm.

We walked into the section as she was picking out more items, so I said, "Huh? Bitch, I'm confused."

"Well, Joe lost the baby by his ex. The girl miscarried or something. She didn't really tell him." Turning around to face me, she smiled from ear to ear.

"Well, why you looking at baby shit for? And so fucking happy. Spill it," I demanded, waiting for her to tell me the news.

"'Cause, sis . . ." She stopped speaking, looked at her belly, then back at me. She rubbed on it with her big, bright eyes.

"Are you *serious?*" I asked, shocked but excited.

She giggled. "Yeah, I'm nervous but excited."

"Aww, I'm going to be an aunty," I said, embracing her and tearing up a little.

"Yeah. Finally, it's my turn," she tittered, sniffling up her happy tears.

Holding her hands and smiling, I said, "Well, don't tell Eric I told you, but we are having another baby too."

"What? Congrats. I thought you was just eating too much," Jalisa said, laughing and rubbing on my belly.

I smiled and thanked her. "Yeah, girl. Thank you. He's excited. He keeps saying it's a boy this time."

"Maybe we'll end up having our babies together. We can be side by side giving birth," she joked.

Jalisa's glow was undeniable. She was genuinely happy, and that's all a true friend could want. We had done enough shopping in the mall and were beginning to get hungry, so we headed out to the parking garage after grabbing something to drink from the vending machine.

"So, Dareen's still alive," I blubbered.

"Wait. Bitch, *what?*" Jalisa almost choked on her Sprite.

Walking outside into the parking lot, I whispered, "Yeah. She's alive. She knows where we live. She's been in Eric's and my house. Eric is working with Detective Peterson to find her."

"That's good. Hopefully, they'll take care of her for good this time. If she survived them shots, she should've been stalking the next nigga somewhere else." Jalisa shook her head, still in a daze from the news.

"Yeah, 'cause if she tries anything like last time, it's going to be way worse for her this time," I told Jalisa with a roll of my neck. Feeling myself getting way too upset, I turned to her and said, "Let's talk about something else."

"Yes, girl, please. That bitch will fuck up a mood, and today has been way awesome," Jalisa chuckled in agreement.

I laughed along with her. "Girl, say that again." I stopped to take a sip of my water.

"So, me and Eric are having a dinner to let everyone know about the new baby in a few days. You know you gotta come."

"That's cool. Girl, you already know I'm showing up," she said, pulling out her car keys.

"You think Joe would want to come with you?" I asked while unlocking my car and starting it with my remote.

Jalisa provided a smile. "Yeah. I think it's time we all officially met. We are family, after all."

"Awesomesauce," I said, finally getting to my car.

"I can't wait for you to meet him officially. I'll send you the details later, after I get home," Jalisa exclaimed while I was unlocking my car door.

"Can we go eat now? I'm starving. Buffalo Wild Wings seems like a move, right?" Jalisa suggested, standing by her car door.

"Cool. I'll follow you, " I told her before hopping into the driver's seat.

Departing the mall, I realized that my best friend was in the best place she'd ever been. I was excited to enjoy the rest of the day with her while Eric was attending to our dear friend, Tommy. What was so odd to me as I drove was that Tommy's girlfriend, Monica, just had a miscarriage as well. Could it be the same person, and we just don't know? I laughed at the thought as the radio blasted "Feeling Myself." I crooned to the song as I went to eat with Jalisa.

Eric

I received a call from Tommy late last night, and he was in tears. He blabbered out that Monica had lost their unborn child somehow. I stayed up all night on the phone with him, trying to console my brother. I never heard him so hurt. I couldn't fathom how he was feeling.

The following morning, Reneece told me she would be hanging out with Jalisa most of the day. Since my wife wouldn't be home and Hailey was with her grandfather, I decided to pop up on Tommy to check on him.

When I got there, Tommy looked horrible. His eyes were swollen and baggy like he hadn't slept in days. He walked me in, beckoning me to follow him to his bar area. Grabbing two small glasses, he poured us both double shots of Crown Royal.

"How you holding up, man?" I asked, taking a sip from the glass.

"We been arguing, and now the baby's gone. Monica said she was going to see her sisters, leaving me here alone. I wanted to be a dad. I knew we were going to be such amazing parents. It sucks, man." Tommy downed his double shot, then poured himself another.

"Tommy, man, give it some time. You'll get better. How's Monica taking it?" I asked, trying to finish my glass.

"I don't know, man. It's weird as fuck. She's weird. One minute, she's okay. The next, she's acting like the world is on her shoulders." Tommy seemed more bemused with his girlfriend's actions, almost as if he had forgotten what she had just gone through.

I tried to help him make sense of the situation. “Well, it could be that way because she just lost a baby. Give her a break.”

“Yeah,” he responded, melancholy.

I patted my best friend on the back. “Look, we’re having a dinner Friday night to make a huge announcement. Bring your girl. We would love to meet her finally.”

With uncertainty, Tommy said to me, “I don’t know if she will want to do that.”

“It’ll be at a restaurant. Just bring her. You both need a night out. I think it will be good for both of you. I’ll text you the info once Neece picks a place,” I said, walking toward his front door.

“All right, I’ll tell her,” he replied, sounding discouraged.

“Cool. Well, hopefully, she’ll come with you. We really want to meet her,” I said, hugging Tommy.

Then I drove back to my home with my wife and daughter. As I pulled out of the driveway, I noticed a car sitting at the edge of the street like they were watching me. I rode past them, wondering if that was Dareen sitting in there.

CHAPTER SEVEN

Dareen

I was saddened to see Eric drive out of Tommy's driveway before I could even catch a good glance at him. I wanted to make sure Eric was gone before I entered Tommy's house. Tommy was standing in the living room watching *Friday the 13th*. When he noticed I was home, he embraced me warmly.

"Hey, beautiful, how you feeling?" he asked after kissing me on the cheek.

"I'm okay. I just needed some fresh air," I responded, breaking away from his grasp to sit on the couch.

"You just missed my boy, Eric. He sends his condolences to us and . . ." Stopping to take a quick sip out of his half-empty glass, he continued, "He's invited us to a dinner they're having in a few days."

I jumped up off the couch, "And what did you tell him?"

"I told him I would tell you about it, and hopefully, we'll make it." Tommy was borderline drunk, wobbling over to me.

"Well, tell him no." I stomped away, heading to the bedroom.

Tommy followed behind me. "Why can't we go? These are my friends. It'll be fun. Please, just one night. You may gain new friends as well. It'll be fun, I promise."

Looking into his beady, drunken eyes, I didn't know what to say. I was about to deny his request. Then I looked into the mirror. My reflection was nodding. I didn't understand why. I wasn't ready to be around the love of my life just yet. The more I stared in the mirror, the more I could see her repeatedly telling me yes.

Finally, I nodded my head, taking a deep breath. "Okay, Tommy. We'll go. But I don't want to stay long."

His whole face lit up like a child on Christmas Day. "Yes, babe. This is going to be great. You'll love them, I promise. Let's go get a drink in the other room, huh?"

Tommy hit my booty before hustling to the other room. I watched him walk away while I stood, looking in the mirror.

The day of the dinner, I was sitting in my apartment, pissed off that Tommy and my other half talked me into this mess. My stomach was in knots. I heard myself say to me, *This night is going to be perfect. Eric is going to see us and realize how much of an ass he's been.*

I screamed out, throwing the pillow with Eric's face on it at the wall. "No!"

"*Listen, tonight is our night. We finally take back what's ours. So, get it together, bitch. We have a busy night ahead of us. And don't forget our gun. 'Cause Eric is leaving with us by* any *means.*" My inner self emerged from the shadows, instructing me for the night.

Listening to myself, I got out of my golden chair to gather my things so I could get dressed at Tommy's.

On my way there, something told me to text my sister Rebecca. I hadn't talked to her in weeks, so reaching out would be nice, just in case things went left.

Me: Hey, Becca. I love you, and I'm headed to a dinner with some friends and shit. If you're not busy, I'll call you later.

Rebecca: Okay, I love you too.

I arrived at Tommy's house around six that evening. When I walked in, he was nowhere to be found until I walked into his bedroom. I could hear the shower running, and Young Jeezy was blasting. I looked over at the bed and saw that Tommy had already picked out an outfit for me. It was a beautiful gesture, and to make my last night with him memorable, I decided to wear the beautiful lavender, off-the-shoulder dress and the gold jewelry he had lying there. On the right side of the dress was a simple diamond ring. I was holding it in my hand when the water in the bathroom cut off.

"Hey, sexy." He kissed me on the neck, pressing his damp, naked body on my back.

"Hey, this dress is beautiful." I turned my head to thank him.

"Well, I hope it fits perfectly," he said, backing away from me. "I'm going to grab a quick drink while you get dressed."

I told him okay as he left me to get ready. Instead of showering and dressing, I lay on the king-size bed and dozed off.

"Hey, babe, you almost ready? We're going to be late," Tommy shouted from the other room, waking me up.

I jumped up. "Tommy, just give me a moment. I haven't even showered yet."

"Monica, you've been in there for two hours. What's going on?" Tommy walked into the bedroom, catching me getting out of bed, still half-asleep.

I walked toward the bathroom. "Nothing. I'm just not feeling right. You should just go. I don't want you to miss it."

"If you don't want to go, I won't go. I'll call Eric now and let them know." Tommy pulled out his phone, and before he could make the call, I stopped him.

"No, baby, we can go. It's fine." I walked into the bathroom and turned on the hot water, steaming up the room.

Staring at my reflection, I wondered how life was going to be with Eric . . . being able to see him, touch him, fuck him every night for the rest of our lives. It was going to be amazing. Even with those thoughts, I started second-guessing going to this dinner . . . until I slapped my face, trying to regain control of myself.

I was getting into the shower, playing my slow jam playlist while I rubbed my Love Spell shower gel across my body, imagining Eric in there with me. As I was daydreaming, Tommy crept in behind me. As he grabbed me from behind, I envisioned him as Eric. We both knew I had a few more days to wait before having sex again, but falling weak to his touch, I allowed him in.

He pushed my body against the shower wall as he entered me gently. I gasped, digging my nails into his back. While making love to me as the water hit our bodies, I moaned his name with every stroke. Tommy was lost in my tight sea when he confessed his love for me. Not saying it back, I continued to moan in pleasure. Before finishing his nut, he bent me over, having me touch the shower walls so he could fuck from behind.

He gave zero fucks that the two weeks hadn't passed. Tommy held my hair as if it were a harness, stroking me deep and hard. He loved how I was moaning his name. It turned him on even more. He slapped my ass as I began to make my ass jiggle on his dick. After we both came together, Tommy washed my body before cleaning himself up.

While he got dressed, I lightly applied my makeup. It had been a long time since I'd seen Eric, so I wanted to make a great impression. I stood in the bathroom, hoping my makeup and hair would give me a different look so that he wouldn't recognize me for the night.

Tommy went back into the living room, allowing me to get dressed. As I viewed my reflection, I knew I was a Bad Bitch. I loved the dress. It fit beautifully, but my mind was racing. My ruby-red bob wig complemented my skin tone perfectly. Tommy was waiting for me in the car. I walked out of the bedroom, wondering if they would recognize me. As I braced myself for this dinner, I got into the car, praying the night would go smoothly.

CHAPTER EIGHT

Dareen

We arrived at the restaurant, and I felt sick to my stomach. I wanted to throw up, but I contained myself. My armpits were sweating uncontrollably. Tonight was not in my control, so not knowing how things would play out worried me.

"Babe, you all right?" Tommy asked as we parked next to a silver Jeep.

"Yeah, I just need a minute. Go ahead and go in," I instructed as I placed my black lipstick from SummerReign Cosmetics on my lips.

Tommy could sense that I wasn't acting normally. "You sure?"

"Yeah, babe, I promise," I lied. I was going crazy in my head. I knew nothing could come out of tonight if things went left.

"OK. If you're not in there in five good minutes, I'm coming to look for you. If you don't want to do this, we can go home. Deal?" Tommy smiled at me.

"We're here now. I'm okay. I just don't want to stay long," I responded, forcing out a smile when I truly wanted to go home.

Tommy pushed my hair out of my face. "Well, regardless of what you may be thinking, you look so amazing."

"Thank you," I replied with a grin.

Tommy kissed my cheek before going inside to show his face. After he left, I had to get my thoughts together. Seeing him go inside, I thought I would chop it up with my best girl: myself.

"Maybe they won't remember me or recognize me," I said, leaning back into the passenger seat.

"*No, you stupid bitch, of course, they will!*" My reflection rolled her eyes at me.

"I'm not stupid," I shouted at myself, grabbing ahold of my hair.

My reflection tossed her hair around, saying to me, "*Come on, let's go.*"

"I'm not going in there. You talked me into this," I said, looking at myself in the rearview mirror.

"*Yes, we are, ho. Come on, bitch, get it together. Go in there and get our man.*" My reflection got me together, giving me the strength to get through the night.

Slowly getting out of the car, I could feel my nerves knotting my stomach. I paced around the car and hesitated before I finally grabbed my purse, locking the door behind me. Before I could smoke a cigarette, Tommy came back out, seeing if I was ready to go in.

I put on my shades, but Tommy tried to take them off, saying it was dark outside. He joked with me, saying that if I walked in with shades on in the dark, they would think I was crazy or hiding something.

We finally entered the restaurant, holding hands. The hostess at the front guided us to the private dining area that had been rented. They informed us that the party was in the back. With my shades still on, hand in hand, we entered the room where everyone was talking and congratulating Joe and Jalisa on something. When they saw Tommy and me walk in, they stopped to greet us.

Reneece tried making conversation with me. "Hey, Monica, right? Have you been here before?"

I didn't want to say anything, afraid my voice would give it away. Tommy responded for me while grabbing my hand. He whispered to me, again asking if I was all right. He reassured me that I was safe around everyone at that table They were all his family. I was talking to Tommy, trying not to show my face when shit hit the fan.

Joe called out my name as I was hiding my face. "Dareen?"

Confused, Tommy looked at Joe. "Nah, you must have her confused with someone else. Her name is Monica."

"Nah, dude, her name is Dareen," Joe said sternly.

I continued to sit there, as quiet as a mouse, trying to hide my face. Tommy leaned over, whispering in my ear, asking what Joe was talking about. I raised my head a tad to look around the table when I caught a glance of Eric and Reneece staring at me. They were wondering if Joe was correct about who I was. Before they could ask me anything, Joe continued his rant.

"Yo, this is crazy. She trying to act like she doesn't know her name now. Or did you tell him your name was Monica?" Joe questioned while he winked at me.

Tommy pushed back his chair. "What, nigga? Didn't you hear me say you got the wrong bitch?"

"Nah, *you* got the wrong bitch," Joe said, shaking his head.

Jalisa begged Joe to sit down and try to get himself together, while Tommy was focused on making them believe I was Monica.

"Babe, please, tell this fool your name so we can get back to the celebration." He waited for me to say something, but I just hung my head.

Tommy started to get annoyed with me. "Monica, gotdamn it, *tell* them," he gritted through his teeth.

I didn't know what to say. I could've lied, but I was made. The man who knew my secret was sitting here at this table, and by the look on Joe's face, he wasn't going to protect me.

"What the fuck are you doing here?" Eric asked me, moving in closer to the table.

"Yo, bro, chill," Tommy said to Eric, tossing his hand in his face.

"No, Tommy. *You* don't get it." Eric's voice grew louder, full of anger.

Joe looked at Jalisa and asked her, "Is she the Dareen who tried to kill you guys last year?"

"Yes," I heard Jalisa whisper back to him.

Tommy sat there, looking confused, then grabbed our menus. I was scared to death my cover was blown, and I had no idea what would happen next.

"I don't understand why y'all keep calling her Dareen," Tommy said, gazing back and forth from the menu to his friends.

"Tommy, remember the girl named Dareen I told you about?" Eric asked, giving me an evil eye.

Holding my hand tightly, he looked up at his friend. "Yeah, I remember."

Pointing his finger at me, Eric said, "*That's* her."

Tommy laughed at Eric, thinking it was a joke. "Nah, man, you just tripping. You said that the girl was dead. Now, she's my girlfriend. You sound crazy."

I sat there avoiding any confrontation until Joe wanted to open up his big-ass mouth.

Joe forced his attention on Tommy. "Did she tell you about losing my baby?"

"*Your* baby?" Tommy asked Joe, stunned. Then he turned toward me with tears in his eyes. "Monica, babe, what's he talking about?"

Joe scooted his chair back, pointing his finger at Tommy. "Man, that bitch name is Dareen, *not* Monica. Stop calling her that fuck shit."

"Joe, shut the fuck up," I shouted, trying to keep him from blowing my cover.

Jalisa jumped into our argument. "Bitch, don't you talk to my man like that."

"Bitch, your ass is lucky I didn't kill you or *her* ass last year," I shouted at Jalisa.

"Fuck you," Jalisa said, standing with a steak knife in her hand. Joe tried to grab Jalisa and take the knife from her. He held Jalisa in his lap, trying to calm her down. As Joe tried to bring some type of peace to Jalisa, I blew my breath, growing tired of all the drama. So, instead, I decided to add more fuel to the fire.

"Joe, I didn't lose the baby. I *aborted* the baby. I had an abortion. I didn't want your fuck-ass bastard child. The only child I want is Eric's." I looked around the table, then locked eyes with that bitch Reneece. "I hope you enjoyed him this past year and some change, 'cause I'm here to get what's mine. Eric, don't you see I did all of this for you?"

Reneece stood up, holding Eric's hand. "We have what you will *never* have. We're having another baby, and here you are, looking pathetic, obsessing over a man you can't fucking have and never fucking will."

I stood up, slamming my hand on the table, yelling, "Yeah? We'll see about that."

I had little time to think about my next move. Tommy was sitting there, stuck on stupid, as Joe yelled, cursing at me. Thinking on my feet while everyone was arguing and distracting themselves about me, I ran over to the high chair and grabbed Hailey, then ran straight out of the restaurant.

CHAPTER NINE

Reneece

Every parent's worst nightmare just occurred. By the time I realized what was happening, Dareen had taken my daughter out of the private room we had.

"Hailey! Hailey! She's got my baby!" I screamed as I jumped up, running behind them. I ran as fast as I could. My baby was in her arms, looking at me, bursting into tears, calling out for me. I was gaining on her when she pushed a cart into my path, causing me to fall.

"Stay here, I got this," Eric instructed as he helped me to my feet. "Someone call 911! Our daughter just got kidnapped," he shouted through the restaurant while pursuing Dareen.

Jalisa and my father stayed with me as I saw Joe go with Eric to get my daughter back. They wanted me to sit there and let them take care of it, but that was my baby girl. Tears streaming down my face, I told them I was going to get her back.

"My daughter!" I yelled, running through the restaurant. "Hailey! Hailey! Mommy's coming!" I kept screaming as I ran behind Eric and Joe.

The hostess at the front told us that Dareen had headed into the parking lot with my child and that 911 was on the way. We ran out to the parking lot, where she placed Hailey on the ground while she broke the window of Tommy's car.

I pointed at our daughter sitting there, screaming as if she were being killed. "Eric, you have to get our baby," I pleaded, trying to keep my tears locked in.

"I can creep up from the back and try to snatch her. Joe can come with me for extra backup." Eric and Joe nodded at each other.

As Hailey cried her heart out, Dareen snapped at her. "Listen, shut the fuck up or I'll kill you just because!"

An elderly woman was getting out of her car when she heard Dareen screaming at my child. She walked over to them and started talking. Seeing that Dareen was distracted, I shot Eric a text telling him to make his move then. Anxiously waiting on him caused my adrenaline to spike.

Eric was about to grab Hailey when Dareen took a piece of broken glass and stabbed the old lady in her neck. I screamed as I saw the woman fall to the ground, holding her neck as it bled out.

Dareen looked at me, then grabbed Hailey from the ground and tossed her in the backseat of the car. She laughed at me before she got inside the vehicle. Eric and Joe tried to open the doors to the passenger seat, but it was too late. Dareen pulled off, leaving them on the gravel. I jumped in front of her path. I knew she was going to hit me if I stayed there, but instead of hitting me, she went around me, slowing down so I could see my daughter's face filled with terror before she sped off.

"She's gone," I said, sniveling as I saw Eric come up behind me.

Eric grabbed me from behind, brokenhearted. "We're going to get her back, I promise."

Now I was sobbing in the middle of the parking lot as Tommy finally emerged from the restaurant, shocked that his car and "his woman" were gone.

When I saw Tommy, I lashed out at him, coming closer to where he stood.

"This is *your* fault. *You* did this."

"Reneece, I didn't know," Tommy declared while holding his head low.

"How could you be fuckin' someone for almost *a whole year* and you don't know shit about her?" I shouted at him before walking away.

Eric had me in his arms, trying to console me when Detective Peterson, six police cars, and two ambulances pulled up. We stood side by side, holding hands, when Peterson approached. I wanted this man out searching for Dareen and our child, not at this damn restaurant.

The police officers started taking witness statements from everyone while the paramedics took care of the innocent old lady who was murdered for no reason at Dareen's hand. As all the commotion was going on around us, Detective Peterson spoke.

"Eric, Reneece, I'm so sorry. But we are going to find Hailey." He hugged Eric, then tried to hug me, but I backed away.

"Bring my daughter back to me *now*. I don't want to hear that 'sorry' shit. Do your job and bring me my daughter," I yelled.

Eric stood beside the detective to talk to him. "Detective Peterson, all we need you to do is to find that crazy-ass bitch."

"Eric, please try to calm down so we can think rationally," Detective Peterson stated, looking at both of us.

Standing up, yelling in the detective's face, I said, "No, *you* don't understand. *Don't* please him or me or tell us to calm the fuck down. That ho has our child. So, don't tell us to calm the fuck down again. I *don't* want to hear that shit."

Eric was holding his emotions together as best he could. But it was hard for both of us to stand here and wait for these fuck-ass police to do their job. There was no telling what Dareen was doing to our child.

Eric stood there trying not to break down. How could he have *not* seen this coming. He should've found her before now. So, Eric went up to Tommy, who was sitting at a nearby corner. He was still trying to piece all that shit together.

"Man, you got to understand if this was you, I would be ready to ride through whatever." Eric tried to talk to Tommy, but with his emotions at a high, he walked away before he took his anger out on him.

"Listen," Joe started, "I can understand and see that you really cared about her. But right now, your friend needs you. We need to help find their daughter."

Joe was trying to reason with Tommy. But Tommy was in a different space. You would think Joe disrespected him the way Tommy's eyes filled with rage. Getting off the curb, Tommy tackled Joe in the parking lot. Eric pushed Jalisa and me out of the way so that neither of us would get hit in their brawl. Then Eric was able to break them up after Tommy elbowed him in the jaw.

Eric turned to Tommy, frustrated, and in tears, he said, "Tommy, I get it, my dude. You hurt, and you're confused, but right now, your brother and your sister need you. Your ho kidnapped my daughter—*your* goddaughter." Eric erupted in tears.

With everyone's emotions at an all-time high, Tommy continued to be a dumb fuck.

"Eric, you just don't—" Tommy was about to make up some type of excuse when there was none, so Eric cut him off.

"Nah, bro, fuck you. Check yo' shit. Help me find my daughter. I don't care if you love that bitch. She's dead when I get my hands on her. She crossed the ultimate line, and you sit here like *she's* the victim." Eric walked away from Tommy to our car.

"Eric," I uttered, following behind him.

He grabbed the gun out of the trunk of the car. "Yeah, babe?"

After he shut the trunk, I stood in front of my husband, looking him deep in the eye. "I know you're going to find her. And make sure when you do that, you bring our daughter home first. Then let me have her. I want to kill that ho—once and for all."

I could tell Eric wanted to keep me away from the craziness, but it was our job to protect Hailey, and we failed. Standing in the parking lot, Eric kissed me goodbye after telling Jalisa to take me home.

Eric was walking away when I called after him. "Eric, bring my baby back alive, you hear me?"

"I will, don't worry," he said before getting into the car with Joe.

CHAPTER TEN

Dareen

I was driving home, and that damn child kept screaming for her mother. I went to my apartment complex, but there were dozens of police cars outside. I made a quick U-turn. I didn't know where to go. I drove around Durham for ten minutes before deciding to park at the Red Roof Inn off Highway 55. I was going to call my sister Rebecca, who stayed near NCCU, but I ended up calling Dawson instead.

After the third ring, Dawson answered. "Hello."

"Hello. Hey, can you get me a room or something? I can't go home. I know the police are already there," I blurted out before I said anything else.

Dawson chuckled. "Dareen, is *that* why you called me? Why would you be afraid of the police being at your apartment?"

Rolling my eyes, I sighed. "Look, man, just help me out. I got his daughter. I just need some place to stay right now and some money."

"What the fuck, yo? You stupid bitch. Why would you kidnap someone's child?" Dawson screamed at me.

"Look, on top of fucking you well, I paid you to make sure I was safe. This is the least you can do," I stated, hoping to jog his memory.

His tone toward me became more aggressive. “Yo, bitch, I don’t owe you shit if you weren’t having my baby. I wouldn’t still be dealing with yo’ trifling ass.”

“Well, lucky for you I killed that piece of shit a few weeks ago, and it wasn’t even yours,” I taunted him, hoping that I struck a nerve.

“Mark my words, you crazy bitch, you’ll get everything you deserve.” Dawson hung up the phone without saying whether he would help me.

The call ended with no resolution. Hailey was still screaming in the backseat. She was working my last nerve. I turned around, yelling at her to shut up, but that just made it worse.

I quickly realized that Dawson wasn’t going to help me. And I never called Rebecca back. So, I shot her a text asking if I could come over for a bit. She sent me her new address, so I headed that way, knowing I would be safe for a little while.

Tommy

We came to my house first. Eric wanted to see if there was anything in my home that could help lead us to her. Once they got out of the car, I stayed in it for a while, trying to get my thoughts together.

When I finally got out of the vehicle, I walked into my house, and Eric was on the phone in my bedroom. I just looked around, feeling sick. Her perfume still lingered in the rooms.

“I can’t believe this shit, man. She never said shit to me about y’all, or who she truly was.” As I began to cry, I shouted, “I can’t believe this shit!” I grabbed a glass off the counter as I walked around the house and threw it at the wall.

"Aye, look, I know it hurts, but you have to keep it moving," Joe stated, leaning on the back of my door.

"You don't know shit. You beat on her. I know all about you, Joe. Does my little sister know you're a woman beater?" I was all in his face, ready for him to hit me, but he just walked away.

"She told you that?" Joe laughed as he backed away from me. "Not once did I *ever* touch her, and it was domestic abuse. Shit, she said *you* were harassing her at her temp job. Guess she played us both."

Looking over my shoulder at this stranger in my home, I said, "What?"

"Everything Dareen said or did was a lie. I didn't know too much about her, but right now, we don't need to worry about what she said to whom or whatever. We need to be there for your homie," Joe stated as he stood in my living room.

Finishing a beer, I shouted, "You *don't* know us."

"Right, but my fiancée is y'all's family. I didn't want to meet y'all like this. I wanted it to be under different circumstances. I'm going to help find his daughter. She's not safe with Dareen." Joe lit a cigar, blowing the smoke in my direction.

Eric walked over to us, coming from my bedroom. "We're gonna meet with my private eye."

"Now?" Joe asked.

"Yeah, I'm ready. Tommy, you still moping around over there?" Eric asked, barely making eye contact with me.

"Man, Eric, come on with that bullshit," I mumbled, sipping my beer.

"If you wanna help me, come on. If you wanna sit here and mope around about this crazy psycho bitch, stay here." Eric grabbed his suit jacket off the chair and walked back outside.

Joe followed behind him, leaving me there to digest everything. Tossing my head back, I felt myself becoming overly emotional. I just wanted to understand why.

I was sitting inside when I received a picture message. I didn't recognize the number, but I knew it had to be Dareen, as they called her. I opened it up, and there was Hailey sitting on a beaten-down tan couch. The poor baby looked terrified. I wanted to do the right thing for her *and* Dareen. I loved them both so much. But instead of going to Eric, I called the number back, hoping to fix it without anyone else getting hurt or killed.

"What, Tommy?" she said, sounding annoyed at the thought of me.

"Why are you doing this?" I asked her, hoping for answers.

"Tommy, just show it to Eric. This is not a game or about you. Don't you get it?" she said.

"Monica, I mean, Dareen, who are you? Please, just tell me the truth," I begged, hoping she would know I was coming from a concerned place.

"My name is Dareen. Tommy, tell Eric he has till tomorrow morning at eight a.m. to meet me at the address in the message, or his precious little girl dies." Dareen hung up without letting me get another word in.

I was so heartbroken and angry. I didn't understand why she was doing any of this. As a man, I never experienced any heartbreak or trauma. I was debating whether to tell Eric about the phone call. Then she sent me an address to meet her. I knew Eric was going to kill her, and I didn't want that. I decided to try to get to her first, to reason with her and get Hailey to safety. If I could save Dareen, we could possibly still be together.

CHAPTER ELEVEN

Eric

I was calling Reneece, telling her to come to Tommy's house so we could all meet with the private eye I'd hired, when I saw Tommy rush out the door. I hurried after him, but I was too late. He was gone.

Coming back into the house, I said, "Joe, did he say where he was going?" I was confused about what was happening.

Joe lifted Tommy's phone. "Nah, but wherever he's gone, it's on this phone. Heads-up."

Joe tossed me the phone, showing me where Tommy had received a text from an unsaved number with an address, and told him to give it to me. I didn't understand why he wouldn't show it to us and just left, unless he had another plan in mind that didn't involve getting my daughter back to me.

Reneece and Jalisa arrived at Tommy's house a few minutes before the private eye got there. I walked outside to greet my wife. I could see that she had been crying. Her eyes were puffy. She had changed into some sweatpants and a T-shirt. Jalisa got out of a separate car.

"Hey, beautiful. You holding up OK?" I asked, kissing her forehead.

"I'm as OK as I will be. So, where are Tommy and this private investigator?" Reneece asked me, noticing Tommy was nowhere to be found.

"I don't know," I said before handing my wife Tommy's phone. "Tommy left his phone, and I don't know if he went here or what the fuck. Dawson hasn't gotten here yet."

Joe came out of the house, greeting Jalisa with a kiss, then looked at Reneece and me. He said, "I don't mean to interject, but you ladies are pregnant. I think you should be far away from whatever happens, but close enough to get your daughter safely."

"No, I want her. I'm going to make her pay. She's taken enough from me; not again this time," Reneece yelled as she sniveled, looking at everyone.

While Reneece was telling me what she *wasn't* going to do, I saw the private eye pulling up. I gathered everyone around so we could all hear the conversation.

"Yo, do you know where my daughter is? Is she somewhere away from Dareen?" I asked, not waiting for him to get out of his car fast enough.

"Hey, Eric. I'm sorry about Hailey." Dawson got out of his car. "To answer your question, I always knew where Dareen was until now," he admitted.

"What?" Eric said, walking closer to him.

Joe walked behind me, going over to the trunk of his car and grabbing a gun out of it. Within the blink of an eye, he shot Dawson in his left leg.

"Now *talk,* nigga!" Joe shouted as he watched Dawson hobble over to his vehicle.

"When I ran into her the first time, I traced the car tags back to Tommy. When I saw her the second time, I tailed her. As fucked up in the head as she is, she figured I was working for the police or you." Dawson leaned on his car, telling his side of the story.

Reneece butted in with her hands on her hips. She rolled her neck, saying, "*And?*"

"Eric, man, listen. Just listen, please. I can explain," Dawson begged, but it went in one ear and out the other.

Getting all in his face, I shouted, "What? She gave you some pussy instead of doing what *I've* been *paying you* to do?"

Dawson grabbed a Kool 100 cigarette out of his pocket, lit it, and looked around at us before saying, "Look, I thought I could help her, change her. I didn't know she was going to do this. I only wanted to protect her 'cause we were having a baby, or so I thought."

"I can't believe this shit," I shouted, punching the driver's side of my car door.

Joe pulled out his gun and aimed it at Dawson. "Fuck that, Eric. I'm done with him."

Dawson held up his hands. "Whoa, man, that ain't necessary."

Reneece walked closer to Dawson. "No, Joe, don't kill him, but he *is* part of the problem." She pulled out her knife and stabbed him in the neck. "Now, that's nothing compared to what your ho's gonna get."

We all stood there in shock at how swiftly Reneece stabbed him. Dawson was trying to grab his gun when Joe caught him. Protecting my wife, Joe fired three rounds into Dawson, letting him fall to the ground, bloody. Joe confirmed he was dead.

Jalisa and Reneece grabbed a water hose, trying to wash away the blood. While they did the easy part, Joe and I grabbed his body off the pavement, stuffing it into the trunk of the car.

"Babe, let's go. If Tommy is there with her, we can get Hailey and then deal with them after she's safe," Reneece said while hovering over Dawson's body and removing the knife from his neck.

"Joe, you and Jalisa can follow behind us. I'll lead the way," I instructed as we left Dawson in the trunk.

"What about the body?" Jalisa asked.

"We'll come back and take care of it later, after Dareen," Joe responded, looking over at Jalisa, then to us.

We arrived at the location and noticed Tommy's car parked on the side of the road. Jalisa and Joe pulled up beside Reneece and me. After finding decent parking, we got out of the car and crept through the neighborhood to find Tommy.

We walked through the neighborhood looking for building 350. Joe noticed Tommy between some bushes, looking into a window. We slowly crept up behind him, trying not to alert him. When we got close, I placed my hand on his shoulder, alerting him to my presence.

"What's up, fam?" I asked, kneeling beside him.

"Eric, what are you—What is everyone doing here? I was going to call you when I had it under control." Tommy sounded nervous as he looked around, seeing all of us there.

"How was you going to call when you left your phone at home?" Joe asked, while showing Tommy, that he had his phone.

"So, that's how y'all found me? I got it covered, so y'all can go," Tommy instructed us as he snatched his phone from Joe.

"Nah, we ain't going nowhere. We do this together or without you. I don't even know if I can trust you," I told Tommy, looking through the window.

All I could see was Dareen and some other person talking. I caught a glimpse of Hailey. Whoever Dareen was talking to seemed not to be up for her bullshit.

Tommy turned around to everyone. "We have to be as careful as possible. I should be the one to deal with Monica . . . I mean, Dareen. No one needs to die."

"Just know your bitch *is* gonna die tonight," Reneece said. "I'll kill you myself if you get in the way. My *daughter's* in there."

"I'm not getting in the way. *I'm* going to kill her," Tommy whispered, not even looking at us.

Reneece backed away from Tommy, saying, "Let's get this bitch then. We need a plan."

My wife was out for blood, and the only thing that concerned me more than Dareen was if Tommy was truly on our side or if he had a plan of his own.

CHAPTER TWELVE

Dareen, Rebecca & Tommy

I was pleasantly surprised when Dareen reached out to me. We had always been so close until our aunt passed away. Things between me, her, and our other triplet, Lana, got so messed up. Lana blamed Dareen for what happened, but I refused to believe our sister was that evil.

As time went on, I left Durham to attend college at Johnson C. Smith, Lana went to Howard, and Dareen went to NCCU. The first two years, we still met up for one another's homecomings, but then one year we fell out over a dude. Things got so bad when I watched my sisters start fighting inside the club.

I stepped in between the two of them, only for Dareen to cut me with the glass bottle she broke on the bar countertop. From that night on, we never spoke again. So, hearing that Dareen wanted to come by with her goddaughter, I was more than excited.

Dareen arrived at my place a little after eight that evening. When she came, I had just ordered some pizza. My doorbell rang, and I ran to open it. And there she stood, and she looked so beautiful.

"Hey, triplet," I shouted, giving her a huge hug before looking down, noticing the little girl who seemed to have been crying. "Hey, princess, I'm Rebecca."

Dareen walked in, letting the little girl run in ahead of her. She walked beside me. "Thanks for letting me see you, sister. It's been awhile."

"Yeah, it has. You know Lana is back?" I responded while locking my door.

"Oh, that ho finally decided to come back to where she felt she was too good for?" Dareen asked sarcastically.

"Dareen, come on, that's not fair." I walked toward the kitchen. "What's your goddaughter's name?"

"Hailey. She's about to be two soon," Dareen said, following behind me.

"I ordered some pizza and wings, so if you wanna eat something or Hailey does, I'm ready." I grabbed some paper plates and cups for the Sprite.

We sat and ate while Hailey watched *Nick Jr.* Dareen was quiet until I asked her about her love life.

"Girl, I met this guy last year named Eric, and we're so in love, but there's this ex he has who won't let him go." She wiped her mouth, then took a sip out of her cup.

"What girl? He must still be fuckin' her or something, that is, unless she's just crazy. Niggas ain't shit these days. Well, most." I stood up, grabbing our plates to throw away.

"He's a great man. Reneece, she just doesn't understand that their time is over, and it's our time. I'm never, and I mean *never,* going to let him go. We even talk about marriage and having a family." Dareen got really stone-faced.

"So, about this Reneece chick, what does Eric say about her?" I asked, curious about why this woman was all in their mix.

"He keeps telling her to leave, or he'll tell me he'll handle it." Dareen checked her phone, then whispered, "Fuck."

"Sis, you good?" I asked her, noticing her demeanor becoming very uptight.

"Yeah. Can you sit with Hailey? I need to take this call. Can I take the call in your bedroom?" she asked as she kept checking her phone.

"Yeah, just go up the stairs to the right across from the bathroom," I directed her.

Dareen ran up the stairs, leaving me with Hailey. I sat beside the little girl, and she looked up at me and said, "Want Momma. Momma," before she cried.

I placed her on my lap to try to soothe her. As she sat there, she drifted off to sleep. Dareen was still upstairs when I turned to the news. There was an amber alert out for a little girl who looked just like Hailey. When they announced her name and age, I realized it *was* Hailey.

I sat in my living room, stunned, unable to believe what I was seeing. Could my sister be the one who kidnapped this little girl?

Dareen

I appreciated my sister's hospitality. It felt nice to be around her for a bit. When she started asking questions about my relationship with Eric, I began to feel a little uncomfortable. I told her the truth about our relationship, but everything else was *not* information she needed.

I started receiving calls from Tommy's business phone while we were talking. He called me several times, so I assumed it was him, not Eric. I had no interest in dealing with Tommy. He served his purpose, so I ignored the calls until I saw the text from his phone.

Tommy: This is Eric. You call me now if you don't want to die right away.

Me: If this is Eric, I'll gladly call back. If not, and you're playing on my phone, it'll be a sad day. I will kill this beautiful little girl. LOL.

I told Rebeca I needed to take a call and went into her bedroom to call Tommy's phone back.

I lay on her plush king-size bed, cleared my throat, and made the call.

"Hello?" Eric's voice sounded so sexy to me, even as angry as he was.

I perked up, hearing his voice. "Hey, baby. You here?"

Eric wouldn't say hello to me or give me any small talk. "Where's my daughter?" he asked, raising his voice at me.

"Come inside, and I'll give you everything you need *and* more," I said, trying to sound sexy.

"Nah, just give me my daughter. Bring her to me," Eric demanded.

"Say please. 'Cause you forget your daughter's life is in *my* hands, baby," I teased him, making sure he knew who was in charge.

"Please," Eric stuttered.

"Great, now, come on," I stated before disconnecting the call.

Before I headed downstairs, I went into my sister's bathroom to make sure I looked sexy for my man. While I was in there, Rebecca hollered up to me that she would be going to the store and left her keys for me to lock up in case we were gone before she got back, which was perfect. I wanted my sister nowhere near some of these crazy people.

Tommy

We saw Dareen leaving the apartment, running to place Hailey in the car. We had to think fast. So, Joe, Eric, and I ran out to the front of the apartment where she was parked.

"Bitch, get away from her now!" Joe shouted, cocking his gun. "Don't make me shoot you."

"Come here." I directed Dareen to our cars.

Reneece and Jalisa were already in their cars, engines running, when we arrived with Hailey and Dareen.

"Why the hell is there a bruise on her?" Eric asked, looking over his daughter as Hailey wailed loudly.

Hailey finally calmed down when Eric rocked her in his arms. He turned away to place Hailey in the car. While he was securing the child inside the vehicle, I took the opportunity to grab Dareen as she stood there.

"I got you, bitch," I said, grabbing her from behind. "Come willingly, or I will blow your fucking brains out."

She stopped struggling long enough to get inside the backseat of Joe's car. Once inside, Joe climbed in beside her, pistol-whipping her until she passed out. We left the parking lot behind, following Eric to drop off Hailey at his father-in-law's. Then we headed to the old warehouse where Dareen held Reneece captive last year.

Dareen was knocked out cold for a while. As we waited for her to become conscious, I sat there staring at her, cracking my knuckles. I could tell by the way Reneece was looking that she was plotting to do some major damage.

Hours later, Dareen finally woke up. She was tied to a chair inside a tin bucket. As she saw everyone who was there, she just looked at us and then began bawling.

"What you crying for? Nobody's buying that bullshit," Joe asked.

I looked around, noticing everyone was in the warehouse. "Why do we need all of you here? Me and Eric would be just fine."

"No, we're all in this together," Joe said, standing beside Jalisa.

Reneece, two months pregnant, walked over to Dareen and punched her in the face. I was so uncertain in my feelings that I turned my head so I wouldn't see what they did to her.

Eric followed behind Reneece, yelling at Dareen, "You keep wanting something and someone you can't have and never will."

"Listen, I'm *not* who you want. I don't know any of you," Rebecca cried out.

"Oh, now you got amnesia? Well, let me show you something," Reneece said.

Reneece walked over to Eric, pulled down his pants, bent over in front of him, and slid his dick inside of her. "That's *my* dick. Now, let me show you."

Reneece began to throw her ass back on Eric's dick. Rebecca turned her head as if she were ashamed. I held her face, making her watch as she shed tears. Eric smiled as he continued to fuck his wife in front of all of us just to piss her off. Reneece was enjoying it herself. She loved making the woman she thought was Dareen watch her and Eric fuck right in front of her.

"Since you like to stalk motherfuckers and shit, you can watch in person now," said Eric.

He then kissed Reneece passionately. Joe and Jalisa walked over to a corner. I was full of questions and anger, and hurt wasn't even in the same mind frame. As Eric and Reneece continued to torture Dareen by fucking each other in front of her, I couldn't hold back anything else anymore.

"This is what you wanted?" I asked. "Are you happy now?"

"Please, I don't know any of you. But, please, let me go. I don't know what you're talking about, *please*." Rebecca pleaded with us, trying to pretend that she wasn't who she was.

"The fuck you mean? You don't know me? I loved you, stupid cunt," I said, pushing her back.

Dareen continued to lie to me. "Tommy, that's your name, right? Please, listen. I am *not* Dareen. Please, don't hurt me." This bitch was pleading for mercy, but I saw right through her.

The more she tried to play with my emotions, the angrier I grew. Everything that happened in the last few hours kept replaying in my head, and I lost control. I pushed her to the ground and gripped her neck tightly until I saw her eyes roll back in her head.

"Tommy, not yet!" Jalisa screamed, but I wasn't hearing anyone.

Joe tried to pull me away, but I elbowed him in his jaw. Eric and Reneece finished dressing and hurried to help Joe get me off of Dareen. I yelled at them that I was cool, then kicked Dareen in the ribs before walking away.

"That ass is ours. I hope you enjoy your last few moments," I said to her.

It was breaking my heart to watch the woman I fell in love with and planned to marry be killed. But Dareen made her bed, and I couldn't help her as much as my heart wanted to.

Before we all departed for the night, Eric told Rebecca, "I hope you enjoy your last night alive."

Her eyes were filled with terror as we walked out. I turned around to look at her petrified face. Eric grabbed my arm, turning me around and guiding me out of the warehouse.

CHAPTER THIRTEEN

Tommy, Eric & Joe

Last night, all I could do was toss and turn. I dreamed of her all night. My heart was shattered, and I had no way to mend it. I couldn't understand how the woman I knew as Monica could be capable of everything she had done. I never once in my life placed my hands on a woman, and I felt terrible for hurting Dareen that way. She didn't deserve that, at least not from me.

The next morning, I woke up and popped an E pill before starting my day. I had no clue where everyone else was. I quickly washed up and threw on some sweats and a T-shirt. I decided instead of meeting everyone later, I would spend my time with her. I was so angry, but I loved her and just wanted to be in her presence.

I walked into the warehouse with a bag of food. I bought Dareen and me something to eat. I had a rough night and didn't sleep well. I couldn't believe I was losing the love of my life this way. When I walked in, she was trying to get her hands loose from the ropes we had bound her wrists.

I crept up from behind, startling her. "Look who's awake."

"Tommy, is that you?" she asked, sounding excited to hear my voice.

"Now you know my name?" I asked, laughing out loud at her antics.

"Hi, Tommy," she said warmly. "Maybe we can talk 'cause you seem more sensible."

I turned my back to her as I opened the can of food. "I brought you some breakfast."

"What's that?" she asked, looking at me with her good eye.

"Your breakfast," I said, showing her the cat bowl full of food.

"The fuck are you giving me—pet food?" she exclaimed ungratefully.

"'Cause you an animal. A human being, a decent one, wouldn't act like you. Now, *eat.*" I forced the first spoonful into her mouth. Dareen spat it out everywhere, with no regard for where the food landed.

I shook off the food that landed on me before backhanding her. "Bitch, eat yo' damn food."

"Why are you treating me like this? I promise I'm telling you the truth, Tommy. Please, let me go," Rebecca implored.

"I'm giving you what you want. You look hungry." I tossed some of the food on her face.

Turning her head from me, she said, "No, you're not. I want you to let me go." Rebecca looked at me with those swollen eyes, almost making me feel sorry for her.

I grabbed the bowl of food, forcing it in her face,

"You better swallow it, or I'm going to shoot you right here," I yelled, pulling out my gun and jamming it into her stomach.

I watched Dareen eat the cat food from the bowl, trying not to vomit as she did so, and tears streamed down her face. The more she claimed to be someone else, the more my heart yearned to believe her.

Eric

Reneece and I spent our morning with our daughter. It felt so good to have her in my arms again. I couldn't imagine life without either of them. Once Hailey went down for a nap, we left her with my father-in-law so we could meet with Detective Peterson. I was pissed at him for not having my back and finding Dareen sooner.

We met up with him around three that afternoon near the Durham Bulls baseball stadium. When we arrived, he was standing in front of his Mercedes smoking a cigar. Reneece and I got out to greet him.

"How's the baby? Hailey? How's she coming along with everything?" Detective Peterson asked, approaching me.

Reneece winced. "She's okay. She's with my dad until we can sort all this out. Keeping her out of harm's way for good."

"I'm sorry. I'm so sorry that you guys are going through this again, especially with kids involved," he said, hugging us.

"Yeah, well, you should've found her sooner," I exclaimed, lashing out my anger toward him.

"Eric, I understand how you're feeling," Detective Peterson said to me, trying to pacify me.

"No, you don't understand. You don't have no kids, remember? Or a wife," I snapped, throwing a subtle punch into his arm.

That struck a nerve in the detective. "I did once, but I lost them due to a case going left. I was too late to protect them. So, trust me, I *do* understand." As he spoke, he looked off into the street.

I apologized to him, feeling myself getting more emotional by the second. I reflected on the past twenty-four hours and realized that all of this was my fault.

I looked back at Peterson and said, "I'm sorry for what I said. I think of what if she would've . . . She could have killed our daughter."

"Eric's right," Reneece said, "Things could've gone bad. Thank God they didn't. We just hope you all will take care of this psycho once and for all."

Detective Peterson agreed with us. Before we departed, he said to us like a concerned father, "Listen, whatever you do, call me when you finish. I understand. Protect your family, and I will make sure it's handled on our end."

We departed from the detective, hand in hand. She was my Bonnie. Tonight, I would make things right for her once and for all.

Joe

Jalisa and I were at home, enjoying every moment together. As much as I wanted my fiancée to stay at home away from the drama, she refused. We spent most of our day in bed. Ginuwine's "So Anxious" played softly in the background as we lay in bed, fondling each other.

She was about to ride me when she stopped looking at me with her beautiful brown eyes. Then she just abruptly asked me, "You don't have any other crazy bitches that'll come after our family or me, right?"

Pulling her closer to me, I softly said to her, "After tonight, no one will have any crazy bitches stalking them.

And I will *never* do that to you. I will protect you and our child forever."

Kissing her neck, then traveling south to her beautiful, full, brown breast, I told her, "Give me my pussy."

She sat up on the bed, tossing her panties on the floor. "Oh, you want this pussy? Come and get it then."

I pulled Jalisa on my face, devouring her succulent juices. She quivered from my tongue flickering against her clit. She gripped the wooden headboard to help her balance as she wrapped her legs around my head.

As she rode my tongue, she climaxed instantly. I didn't stop after her first nut. I continued to eat her, hoping to make that juicy, sweet pussy purr more and squirt all over my face.

Her body began to quiver uncontrollably. I knew she was ready to squirt for me. I held her down on my face, gripping her phat ass cheeks as tightly as I could, sucking on her pearl harder until she came over me. Then I slid her from my face onto my long, thick dick.

I filled her pussy with my dick, thrusting it deep into her. I pumped Jalisa faster and faster until we came together. After the climax, I lay her on her right side, kissing her deeply.

"I can't wait for tonight. All of this will be over. Especially for my sis, you know?" Jalisa ran her fingers through my dreads slowly while we lay in each other's arms.

"Yeah, I feel you. Everyone will be done with this—and her," Joe said, pulling Jalisa closer. "But right now, I need some more of my fiancée."

I slid inside of Jalisa once more, slow stroking her from the side. Her soul was intertwined with mine. I made love to her as if this were the last time we would see each other alive. Cherishing every piece of her pregnant, naked body, I was in complete bliss.

After having a nice, sensual afternoon with my fiancée, it was time for all of us to meet up at the warehouse. From what I could tell, none of them were true killers like me, but they hated her so much that they would do anything to get rid of Dareen.

When we walked into the warehouse, we all smelled the foul odor of feces and piss. Tommy was pacing the floor back and forth like a madman. He was still on his sappy shit. He had sat in front of Dareen and asked her, "Did you ever love me?"

Dareen belted out, "Tommy, I told you before, and I'll repeat it. I love no man but Eric."

Tommy punched her in her jaw and said, "Don't say that shit to me again!"

"Tommy, sweetie, you're still overthinking," she said. "I can't tell you I love you, 'cause I don't know you or any of you. I keep telling you that I'm *not* her. You *have* to believe me."

Tommy took the gun out of his gym bag, slapping Dareen in the face over and over again, crying out, "You liar." Before he could do too much damage, Eric and Reneece walked in.

"Tommy, chill, brah." Eric grabbed his hand.

"I knew you would believe me. Tommy, *please,* save me," Dareen whispered, looking up at everyone with her swollen left eye.

"Bitch, ain't nobody saving you," Reneece said sharply.

"Man, fuck this ho," I yelled, getting ready to pull my gun out when Jalisa touched my hand.

"It's not time yet," Jalisa whispered to me.

"Please, you all have to believe me! Tommy, *please,*" Rebecca petitioned, hoping Tommy would fall for it.

Reneece looked down and saw the cat food cans. "Yo, babe, he fed that ho cat food," she said, laughing, after gaining Eric's attention.

"Well, she has such a friendly pussy, I just thought she would like to eat like one," Tommy responded with his face stone cold, staring at her.

After all the jokes were done, Eric stood in front of the person he thought was Dareen. "Now, it's time for you to feel the pain you caused us."

CHAPTER FOURTEEN

Reneece

Joe and Jalisa arrived around seven o'clock. They walked in with tons of cleaning supplies, trash bags, bleach, and gasoline. I was standing in a corner, talking to Eric, still clowning at how Tommy made Dareen eat pet food when I heard my best friend's loud-ass mouth come in.

"Hey, why does it smell like piss in here?" I heard Jalisa yelling as she and her boo entered.

"Y'all let the bitch piss on herself?" Joe asked as he guided Jalisa farther into the warehouse.

Tommy nodded, while I enjoyed a laugh at Dareen's expense. She wanted to make a fool out of us, but instead, she was now the fool. Eric tossed a duffel bag full of different knives and guns on this steel table that was in the middle of the floor.

"Y'all sure you're ready to do this? Especially you, Tommy. We need to know that you're with us all the way and still not fantasizing on what y'all could have been and shit," Eric said as he looked around at every one of us.

Quietly, everyone nodded in agreement, even Tommy. However, something felt off, but I couldn't put my finger on it. I just figured it was nerves. Never had I killed someone before, but Dareen would damn sure be my first and only kill. And I planned to make it worth my while.

I looked at my husband and said to him, "Well, let's go ahead and dead this bitch, and then it's time, babe."

"Shit, my new friend, I am *always* ready. I even have a machete in the trunk of my car," Joe responded with a huge smile on his face.

Jalisa raised her hand. "Let me go first. I think Reneece and Tommy should be the ones to finish it. They've suffered the most from this crazy psycho."

"Man, I don't fuck care who does what," Tommy yelled. "I just want this bitch dead, ASAP."

Dareen opened her eyes slightly, as if she were sleeping the whole time. I just wanted to shoot her in the head, but I also wanted her to be tortured. I wanted her to feel so much pain that she couldn't help but beg for death. Then I was going to kill her . . . slowly and softly.

Dareen was looking at all of us, barely saying a word. She and Jalisa locked eyes.

Rebecca lifted her head. "You know what? When I come out of this, I hope you all know there will be repercussions for your actions toward me. I told you I am not who you are looking for. Please, let me go."

Jalisa had had enough of Dareen's bullshit. I had never seen my bestie so infuriated. With the blink of an eye, Jalisa picked up the hunting knife, stabbing it into what she believed was Dareen's eye.

"Bet you can't see shit now, you stupid ho. This a game? This is all a game, *right?*" Jalisa said, taunting her.

Joe grabbed Jalisa, leaving the knife dangling from her eye. Once we had calmed Jalisa, we walked away from Dareen so she couldn't hear our discussion. Where we stood on the ground was an old bloodstain from the very spot my brother blew his brains out. Everyone was talking, but I just zoned out. After everyone agreed to the plan Eric had described, we turned around, ready to make the first move, but Joe couldn't wait.

"Please, please, don't hurt me anymore. I'll do whatever, just don't hurt me," Rebecca begged.

"Shut up, ho. He ain't buying your game," Joe said, quickly snatching the knife from her eye.

Rebecca yelped out for help while Eric put on his gloves, taking the knife from Joe. Eric then stabbed her in the left side of her abdomen. Twisting it slowly and digging it as deep as he could, he whispered to her, "This is for all the pain you caused us and for hitting my daughter."

I made eye contact with Eric, nodding, letting him know I was ready. I grabbed a pair of plastic gloves while Eric waited for me. Hand in hand, we walked up to her, pushing the knife deeper into her left side. She screamed in agony as Eric crudely yanked out the blade. Her blood flowed out and stained the cracked cement floor as she eyed Tommy.

I could tell she was plotting something. I hoped that while we were away, Tommy didn't fall for the shit and become her fool once more. I was so enraged with the thought of her presence still lingering among us, and I was so ready to get this over with. Tommy dropped the knife on the cement floor as his hands trembled. I picked it up and held it while watching them.

"You caused so much grief, and now, Karma has come to give it back to you full circle. You think you can just do whatever you want and nothing will happen to you? You took innocent lives and played with people's hearts. Your time is up, bitch," I screamed.

Rebecca started, "I know one of you *has* to believe me. Do you think I would be begging y'all asses to let me free if I were her? Tommy, umm, Eric, Reneece, all of y'all want me to die like this? Want me to die for some shit I know nothing about? *Please!*"

Eric and I waited for Tommy to make a move, but he was stuck on stupid. So, Eric started to head in Tommy's direction when I held his hand. I figured he needed to hear a more subtle voice than Eric's cussing and yelling at him.

"Tommy," I said walking over to my friend, "she means you no good. Think about everything she's done. She's just still trying to use you. You can't save her, and as much as you may love her, you have to let her go."

"Tommy, *please,* be the voice of reason. My name is *not* Dareen. One of you has to believe what I'm saying is true. Please! I don't know what she did to all of you, and I can't fix it, but killing me *isn't* going to fix it. I'll help you find her, just please," Dareen implored us. "Tommy, if she broke your heart, I can mend it. I know how it feels to be betrayed by someone you love. Please, help me."

"Shut up!" Joe screamed before spitting in her face.

When Tommy heard her say those words to him, something changed with him. I wanted him to be a man and unleash his wrath upon her. But Tommy was bitching out. I guess this nigga was still in love.

With tears streaming down his face, he said, "I can't do this." He turned away. Rebecca screamed for Tommy to help, but he never did.

Dareen looked at us with her one eye and said, "Please, please, don't kill me. I'm begging you, *please,*" she screamed, but her wishes fell on deaf ears. It was my turn now.

I looked at the hunting knife in my hand and pricked my finger with the top of the sharpened blade. As Rebecca shook her head no, I just smiled as I made my way to face her.

"This is for my mother and my little sister that you killed that day in the mall," I shrieked while stabbing her repeatedly three times in her stomach. I stopped for a moment to look upon this being who had caused my family and me so much pain. Closing my eyes, I could visualize that moment when my brother killed himself, and my daughter was kidnapped. Those visions ignited a red-hot blaze inside me. I yanked the knife from her belly. Now, I pressed the tip of the blade against her throat, and then I said to her, "This is for my brother and for Hailey. You will no longer bother my family or me. I hope you rot in hell where you belong." Slowly, I slit her throat.

After watching her blood drip from the knife, I stepped back, laughing insanely. She looked like a fish out of water, gasping in her last moments of life. I leaned over, whispering in her ear, "Goodbye, bitch," before stepping back to watch her bleed to death.

CHAPTER FIFTEEN

Tommy

It was done. No matter how I tried to compress the bleeding, it wouldn't stop. After her pulse faded, I screamed out in agony. I allowed my anger to overpower my heart and love for her. I thought it was possible to save her, but now, it was too late. I walked outside where Joe and Eric were. I felt like shit, and I thought Eric would've talked to me to make it better.

"It's all over, Tom." Eric patted my back and stood beside me.

"Is she dead?" Joe asked, while looking at me as my lip quivered.

"Yeah." I folded into my best friend's arms, sobbing.

"Tom, listen," Eric said, "all of this was for a reason. Everything happens for a reason, you know? We may not know now, but soon, it will be revealed."

"Yeah, man. What's the reason for this shit?"

"Tommy—"

"Nah, man, maybe we should've just taken her to the police," I uttered as I searched for my lighter.

"And have her escape again?" Eric asked while snickering, "Yeah, right. We did the right thing, like Spike Lee."

"We don't know that. What if we didn't even kill her? What if whoever that was told the truth? What if Dareen just wanted to make amends? Huh? So many questions you can't fucking answer."

"Tommy, don't let that love shit fool you about her. She wasn't the one for you," Joe added while we all stood outside.

I moved away from Eric. "You don't know that. I *could've* changed her. She could have changed. Y'all didn't give her a chance to redeem herself."

"Bro, I'm going to say this one last time," Eric said, tossing his cigarette to the side.

"Say what?" I asked.

"She kidnapped my daughter, she used you, almost two years ago, she kidnapped Reneece, and broke out of jail. She killed Reneece's sister and shot her mother. So, nah, nigga, you should be happy we deaded that bitch." Eric got all up in my face.

I took a deep breath. "Yeah, whatever."

"Did she tell you she killed her only friend? She killed her 'cause she wouldn't help her kill Reneece. So, you bitching 'bout some pussy that ain't worth bitchin' 'bout. Shake this shit off and take the time you need. You'll find someone for you," Eric shouted while pushing his finger against my head.

"Let's just get this body out of here. I'll deal with this shit on my own because you don't understand," I said, walking away from my best friend.

I went back inside, removing her lifeless body from the chair where we had her tied. I rocked back and forth, holding her in my arms. As I moved a strand of red hair from her face, Joe appeared out of nowhere with his machete and pulled her out of my grasp. I tried to pull her back, but Eric held me.

"You don't have to do this. Man, *stop!*" I screamed, trying to break free from Eric.

I looked at Joe. "What are you going to do to her? Stop it," I shouted at him. "Leave her alone!"

"Easier to get rid of the body this way, so just chill out," Joe said to me as he covered his face, preparing to dismember Dareen.

"I do *not* want to her body chopped up like some piece of meat," I said, fighting back the tears.

Eric kept holding me. "It's the best way, bro."

"This is about all of you. You don't give a damn what I fucking want," I shouted, elbowing Eric in his stomach.

"No, we aren't doing what y'all want anymore. This is *my* decision," Eric yelled at all of us.

Rolling my eyes, I looked over at Reneece. "Yeah, Neece."

Reneece came up beside me. "Listen to me. We all know you're hurting. I understand you're hurting. But you must understand, when it came to her, it was either her or us. One day, when you're ready, we'll explain what happened a year or so ago, and why this decision was so easy for us."

"Yeah, you told me already." I blew off Reneece, not trying to hear their story all over again.

"Yeah, pieces. *Not* everything. You don't know what she's done to us," Reneece shouted.

"Y'all ain't got to dismember her like a fucking animal, though," I shouted back, standing in front of Dareen's body.

Reneece reached out to me. "Tommy, look—"

"Nah, man, come on. She was still a person," I interjected, hoping they would see my point.

"Look, we have a final step. Get rid of the body. We get rid of her completely and go back to life," Reneece calmly told me.

"What kind of life would that be?" I asked, trying to understand. "She's dead already."

With his machete in hand, Joe swung, and, limb by limb, he chopped her up. After he finished, he tried coming up with a different way to get rid of her parts. Her limbs were scattered over the warehouse floor. Joe's idea to get rid of Dareen was to burn her in the incinerator before leaving. That way, no evidence would be left behind.

"You trying to be funny?" I asked with an attitude.

"Nah, nigga, you still actin' crazy over here. Remember, she played you, making you think she wanted your ass," Joe said, picking up pieces of her chopped-up body.

I pointed my gun at Joe. "Nigga, try me again. I'm tired of yo' mouth."

"Nigga, if you gonna shoot me, shoot me. You ain't got the balls. And honestly, I think you shouldn't have been involved because you worried about this ho instead of your homie and his family. Priority's messed up," Joe lashed out at me, pissing me off more.

"I will if you burn her body. We've done enough. I'll take care of the remains—*not* you." I was still holding my gun.

"Fine. You do it." Joe walked out of the warehouse, leaving me with her remains.

After watching them dissect her body, I was so disgusted. I couldn't stand to look at her body that way. I finally walked outside and saw Joe and Jalisa standing by their car, talking.

Joe looked out over the parking lot. "There's nothing else to worry about. We got rid of her."

"I know," Jalisa murmured as her head hit Joe's left arm.

Joe then told Jalisa, "No one will ever hurt you or our child. I promise. My word is bond."

"I know, Joe. No worries. We just have to focus on the wedding and our baby." Jalisa puckered up on him.

I overheard Jalisa and Joe's conversation, which only made me more upset. Here everyone was with their happily ever after, and what I thought was mine was just dismembered right before my eyes.

CHAPTER SIXTEEN

Eric & Dareen

After leaving the warehouse, Reneece and I decided to visit Detective Peterson. She convinced me it would be good to give him a heads-up, just in case something came back about that night. Even though I was ready just to let it all be over with it, she was right. So, I called him before we went to pick up Hailey, and he agreed to meet us. Around midnight, we met Peterson downtown in the parking lot of Blue Café.

"Eric, Reneece, is everything OK? I've been looking everywhere for you two," Detective Peterson said as we approached him.

"Yeah, everything's good," I replied, hoping not to have to go into detail about what happened earlier that night.

Detective Peterson didn't hesitate to figure out what was going on. "Have you heard or seen Dareen? Has she popped up or anything?"

I just held my wife's hand as I told him, "We won't be hearing from her again. And I mean *ever* again."

"Good. No need to keep the case open then. I'll close it and add notes detailing that all leads went cold. The good thing is, everyone is alive and safe," he stated.

"Yes. Yes, it is," Reneece said, looking up at me with a smile.

I gently smiled and said, "All right, well, we need to head home. But we'll talk to you later."

Detective Peterson bid us farewell. After he shook my hand and kissed Reneece's cheek, he told us how happy he was that we had finally ended everything.

"You think Tommy is going to be okay?" I asked her as we approached her father's home to pick up Hailey.

"With time. With time, babe. And he knows we will be here for him," Reneece reassured me while holding my hand.

"Yeah, I hope he remembers that," I said with a heavy sigh.

After picking up Hailey, we went straight home. It was the longest day of our lives. When we finally entered our home, I decided to shoot Tommy a text before showering with my beautiful wife.

Me: Tommy, listen. Remember, no matter what, I'm your brother. Thank you for having our backs, even though it was hard for you. Love you, bro.

Tommy never replied. I was going to call, but I'm sure he just needed some time. After Hailey passed out in our bed, Reneece and I took a shower before heading to bed ourselves.

Reneece looked over at me. "Everything is going to be so much better now."

"It definitely is. Our lives are only going to get better from here," I replied, pulling her into my arms.

I lay in bed with my pregnant wife and our little girl, realizing that the most precious gifts I had were right next to me. Now, our lives could truly be at peace, and I couldn't feel any better about it.

Dareen

I followed them when they took my sister. After that, I would just pop up and check the scenery. This day, I was going to attend to her wounds and attempt to get her out of there. I waited for everyone to leave, but Tommy still stuck around. I sneaked into the warehouse while Tommy sat in his car. Walking in, I discovered my sister's body all chopped up. I instantly got sick to my stomach and vomited in a nearby corner. I felt bad that I didn't make it in time to save her.

I didn't realize they'd taken her until the phone stopped ringing and all the text messages from Tommy stopped. Standing near her body after spitting out the puke, I whispered, "Thanks, Becca, for taking the hit for me. You were always the kindhearted one."

I was going to gather her limbs and place them in a bag when I saw Tommy come back inside. There was an incinerator in the left corner of the room. I ran toward it and crouched down beside it.

Tommy was taking a bottle of something to the head as he made his way over to my sister's body. He took her right hand and placed it on his chest.

"I wish I could've saved you. I loved you, but you didn't love me. I would've done anything for you. I love you, Dareen. I fell in love with the beautiful person you were to me, my Monica. I don't know if it was a lie or if that was truly you, but I hope you find peace."

Tommy started to cry as he gathered her body. He placed them all except that hand inside the incinerator. I watched him in the shadows mourn over me, and that is when I realized that Tommy was still my way to get to all of them. My journey was far from complete. The revenge I was going to exact wasn't going to be for Rebecca, but for all the injustices done to me. And Tommy was going to be the one to help me. He just had no idea . . . and never would.

Delusions of a Side Chick

Part 2

PROLOGUE

Dareen

After my sister Rebecca was murdered, I needed a new refuge. Rebecca's death would not go in vain. She not only saved me but also gave me enough time to get rid of all of them, one by one, until no one was left but Eric and me.

After leaving the warehouse, I went back to my sister's apartment to see if I could find her phone. As I walked into her empty apartment and closed the door, I took a good look at her place. There was a picture on her television stand, in a cherry wood frame, that looked familiar. I walked closer to it. It was a picture of our high school graduation day. We looked so happy back then.

I brushed my finger against my sisters' faces before placing the picture back. Then I walked into the kitchen to make something to eat. After eating, I went into her bedroom and fell asleep on her king-size bed. I awoke the following morning, realizing Rebecca was never coming back. I had to get those fools back for killing my sister. The fact that they entertained the thought of killing me so easily was hilarious. They should've known I wouldn't have gone down without a fight.

I turned on Rebecca's forty-two-inch flat screen to see if anything was said on the morning news. There was no mention about finding dead bodies in a warehouse on the five thirty, the six o'clock, and the seven a.m. news. It was like it never happened. I decided I would reach out to my other sister, Lana. I had to think of a good lie to tell her ass.

While I tried to get all my thoughts together, I went downstairs to make some coffee. While I was on the stairs, someone knocked on the door, which shook me. I didn't know whether I should answer it, so I just stood there, listening to the knocks, till my inner self told me to answer it. Coming closer to the door, my heart pumped faster and faster.

"Who is it?" I yelled through the door without even cracking it.

"Man, Becca, come on and answer, babe. I miss you," a female voice shouted back.

"Who is it?" I asked again, trying to figure out who was behind the door.

"Becca, it's me, babe, Kiesha. Please, let me in. I just wanna talk, okay?" the woman said, sounding remorseful.

"*Bitch, let that ho in. She may be useful,*" I heard myself tell me.

"But how? What if she realizes I'm not Rebecca? Then what do we do?" I asked myself. I needed a plan and had no real time to come up with one.

"*Listen, stop actin' like a punk-ass bitch. We raised you better than that. She acts funny, we kill her and get rid of her ass. Then we use her as the scapegoat with Lana. We got this. Now, get our pussy pleased by this ho and dead her,*" my inner self instructed me.

I wasn't one to disobey myself and her requests. That could be bad. So, obeying the orders given to me, I tried to straighten myself up some, then answered the door. I opened the door slowly, and this pretty-ass stud stood in front of me. Her sexy ass reminded me of a Puerto Rican version of Young M.A. I wanted her to pull out her strap, bend me over, and fuck me like the nigga she wanted to be.

"Baby, listen, I'm sorry. Like, I know it's been a few weeks. But I promise you, she didn't mean nothing to me. I was just unsure about you. I mean, I was unsure about my feelings. Fuck, I'm messing this up." Kiesha came inside, rambling on and on, making no sense.

The more she talked, the more I wanted to know how good those succulent pink lips would feel wrapped around my pussy lips. The more my thoughts ran wild, the wetter my pussy got. I sat on the bottom step, not paying attention to anything else this girl, Kiesha, had to say.

"Kiesha, wanna show me you're sorry and honestly make this work?" I asked, while slowly rubbing my thighs together and biting my bottom lip seductively.

"Rebecca, babe, I'll do anything, just name what you want. I'll do *anything* if you'll take me back, please," she pleaded.

Damn, as much as she begged, she must've really fucked up. I just wanted her to shut the fuck up and eat my damn pussy.

I took off my shirt, revealing my naked body, and motioned for her to get on her knees. "Eat this pussy, and then we'll talk about what else you can do. Just right now, I want your lips to talk for you," I said, and she smiled like a kid at Christmas. Kiesha dove into my pussy headfirst, and from the first suck on my clit, I knew I was in for a good time.

CHAPTER ONE

Tommy

A Year Later . . .

My life hasn't been the same since the night we killed Dareen. Part of me wished it was all a bad dream and the love of my life was back in my arms. I decided about five months ago that I should probably see a psychiatrist to help with the pain. This whole situation was so fucked up.

This morning, I was to meet with her for our regularly scheduled session. I met with Dr. Lana three times a week, as often as I needed. Between her, the antidepressants, and the alcohol, I've been trying to manage my life. I haven't been the best partner to Eric for our business, but my mind was so focused on who I thought was Monica.

I arrived at her office around ten this morning. Once I parked, I tried to find some cologne to mask any stench of alcohol. She always seemed to tell when I've had vodka for breakfast. I went into her office, hoping I looked as normal as possible since she was trying to put me in AA meetings. I waited for about ten minutes before I was allowed back to see her.

The session started like usual. "How are things since I last saw you? Any improvements?" etc. Even though I needed to see her, I felt off. Truth be told, I haven't been sleeping well. Monica, I mean Dareen, was everywhere. I couldn't close my eyes without envisioning her in bed with me, or her chopped-up body lying in front of me. I started to tell Dr. Lana about my dreams after I confessed how much I loved and missed her, but she started looking at me like I was going insane.

"Doc, I know what you could be thinking, but I'm not going crazy, man," I said to her before sipping my water.

"Seems like you are. I think you should still see me three or four times a week, at least until I can see more progress," she suggested while writing in her leather notebook.

"I ain't crazy or going crazy. I'm perfectly fine." I was trying to convince her and myself at this point. I knew I was losing it more and more every day. I felt it.

"Then why do you say that you can't sleep at night? These wild dreams and hallucinations are the cause, don't you think?" she questioned as she looked at me with her big brown eyes, reeking worry.

"They are just nightmares. Regular people have them all the time, Doc. No need to get all hype," I explained, hoping she would just drop the topic.

"Constantly?" She paused. "How often do you have them?" she continued while looking at me with her eyebrows raised.

Leaning forward from the black suede chair, I turned to the doctor, realizing my time with her might end sooner than usual. I didn't want to tell her or anyone about the dreams I've been having about Dareen.

Even though it's been a year, Dareen and my love for her haunted me. I missed the woman I was in love with. At some point, I had to realize there were two different personas involved. Shit, the whole thing still baffled me. But one thing was clear: I still loved this woman.

I had changed into a completely different person over the past few months. I didn't want to be near anyone, and I didn't feel the need to live any longer. I felt like my whole world had come crumbling down. Like the great R. Kelly said, "If I could turn back the hands of time, things would be so different." My relationships with all my friends, especially Eric and Reneece, had changed drastically.

My therapist kept trying to get me to talk, but I wasn't in the mood. I wanted to let it all out, find a shoulder to cry on, but I knew I couldn't say too much without incriminating myself or my friends. Some things were better left unsaid. I was struggling to find who I was before Dareen came into my life. . . before all this anger, bitterness, and depression took over my life.

I turned to face my therapist. She was about my age and, to be honest, I was starting to feel like I needed someone with more experience. I decided to leave, but before I could walk out, she stopped me. She reassured me of her so-called true intentions, saying she felt she might need to see more of me to help with my healing process and shit.

"Tommy, why don't you schedule an appointment for me anytime tomorrow? I will rearrange my calendar." She offered to let me see her for an extra day, which was sweet and all because I knew it came from a good place, but I wasn't feeling it.

"Doc, I know you wanna help. But maybe this was a mistake." I stood up, getting myself together and dismissing myself.

"Tommy, you say that every time, but here you are. I just want to help," Dr. Lana calmly said to me.

"Aye!" I said, raising my voice. Then I took a step back and a deep breath before speaking to her, "I know I need to try to be open more. But over the past few months, I haven't been opening up to anyone, not even you. So, I'm sorry, but it feels like a waste of time and money."

"Tommy . . ." she said, trying to get me to sit back down. "Listen, I want to be here for you. You have all my numbers. Just call me. *Please.*"

I nodded and told her OK. Without turning back, I gathered my keys and jacket and left her office. Walking through the garage, I let out a scream filled with agony. As I walked, I punched one of the walls out of pure anger as I had flashbacks of that night my friends and I murdered Dareen. When I finally reached my car, I got in quickly so I could talk to my best friend, Effen Vodka.

While I finished the last shot in the bottle, I reached into my glove compartment, pulling out a picture of Dareen I had made. Just looking at her big, beautiful eyes and that sideways smile melted my heart. I missed her so much. They didn't know the woman I knew. Dareen may have deserved some things, but not death.

I placed her picture on my chest and bawled like a big baby. Every time I saw her face, it was like losing a piece of me over and over again. I reached for my bottle of Jose Cuervo from under my seat, taking it straight to the head. As the bottle departed my lips, I saw her. She looked so real. I shook my head, trying to shake her image, thinking it was just the liquor fucking with my head. But she was still there . . . standing in front of my car with her swollen eye and slit throat. It was too much to bear.

Honking my horn, I screamed out of my window, "No, you're not here! You *aren't* real."

I shut my eyes, then reopened them slowly—and there she was, right at my window. She waited for me to open my eyes. Once I did, she said, "Tommy, I am real. I'm not going anywhere."

"Go away! Go away! This is your fault," I shouted while rolling my windows up.

Dareen slammed her hands on the hood of the car, screaming, “How, Tommy? I just wanted to be loved. You were supposed to love me. And look what you did!”

I took another shot of tequila. When I looked back around, she was gone. I placed the cap back on my Jose before sliding the bottle in between my legs. Dareen was haunting me. I could’ve saved her. I *should’ve* saved her. But I didn’t. I knew that’s why she was there.

Driving off from my therapist, I realized the person I was in love with had so many secrets, lies, and was completely different from what I saw when I was with her. My emotions overtook me, and I cried as I hit the gas. I sped home doing ninety-five on the freeway.

I slowed down just enough to keep from getting pulled over. Finally, home, I stumbled inside my quiet house half-drunk and heartbroken. I walked through my home, throwing my keys on the floor. The ghostly scent of the Victoria’s Secret perfume she wore still lingered in the doorway. I walked through the hallway into my bedroom, imagining Dareen lying in the bed.

I slammed my bedroom door, turning around and going into the kitchen. Opening the refrigerator, I grabbed a two-day-old plate of Chinese. I didn’t even smell it to make sure it was good. I just threw the plate in the microwave and walked away.

As my food warmed up, I made a quick call to Joe. As much resentment as I had toward him, he was marrying someone I considered my little sister, so the least I could do was be cordial. He didn’t answer my call, but he texted me moments later.

Joe: What’s up?

Me: I need some more plants.

Joe: I got you. I’m not far from you. I’ll swing by in like fifteen mins.

Me: Cool.

I made my way into the kitchen to grab my food. Lifting the dish rack, I took a small envelope from beneath it, wrapped in a plastic bag. I opened it slowly to see the picture I had printed off my phone of the late Dareen. She was in one of my black dress shirts, standing in my kitchen, sucking some icing off her finger. She just looked so beautiful at that moment. She wore no makeup, her hair was messy, but she was just a natural beauty. I couldn't help but take a picture.

My doorbell rang, startling me. I caressed the picture before giving it a soft kiss. Placing the picture back in its safe place, I took a deep breath and went to the door. Not a moment went by that I didn't miss her. I even hoped deep down inside that we killed the wrong person so I could get my love back and make things right.

CHAPTER TWO

Dareen

I had been staying with Lana off and on since Rebecca's murder. I'd come to her one night after a heated argument with Kiesha. After I allowed her to give me a black eye and a few other bruises, I reached out to my sister through Twitter, hoping she would respond. When she did, I showed her my wounds and told her we needed to meet. She came over to Rebecca's apartment that same night, and I gave her this whole fake, drawn-out story. I was quite tickled by her reaction when I told her how Eric got jealous of Tommy being with Rebecca, and that they had a big fight, even though he was married. Then I explained how I tried to save her and how they tortured us both and made me watch them kill our sister right before my eyes.

Man, Lana was livid. I had never seen her so hurt or angry. I told her I was coming up with a plan to get them all back, and before I could ask if she would help, she had already decided she wanted in. The way my mind works, I'm a genius. Before long, we had decided that if we separated the crew, then they could be picked off one by one. Tommy was first on my list. In all honesty, I didn't want to kill him. I knew he would never really hurt me. But I knew I could get him to turn on his bestie.

It started off with simple little things. I started staking out his home when I noticed that he wasn't going into the office. It seemed as if he was troubled by "my death." He was such a sad case, but I was genuinely enjoying his pain. Tommy looked as if he hadn't showered in weeks. He probably had salty balls. After observing him for some time, I went back to my sister with all the details. She informed me that he could be suffering from depression. That's when we came up with the idea of Lana being his therapist.

I gathered a stack of my sister's business cards and left them in places he would find them. My sister was getting more and more clients, but not from those that we wanted. It took us dropping business cards near his home twice a week, placing posters in the park where he would take his morning and evening runs, pamphlets at the Starbucks he went to every morning, and we even got a billboard made. It was exhausting, but after a while, it paid off. Two months of doing that shit nonstop, he finally caved in. I was elated when I saw his name set up for a session.

It was about seven that evening when Lana finally came home from work. I heard her keys rattling at the door like she couldn't get in. When she finally walked through the door, I wasn't sure what to expect. Lana kicked her patent-leather red pumps into the middle of the hallway adjacent to her living room, where I was sitting watching *Family Feud.*

"Well, how did it go today?" I asked, acknowledging she had come home.

"Damn, Dee. First of all, I just walked into the house from a very long day and crazy-ass traffic. Second of all, since this is *my* home, and you *aren't* my man, you could at least greet my ass. Thirdly, I'll tell you what I have from Tommy when there's something to tell. I explained that already." Lana responded with an attitude seeping from her words.

"Aye, check your attitude," I shouted, turning my body slightly toward where she was standing.

Lana began laughing like I told a joke. I didn't understand what was so funny. I gave her my middle finger, then went back to watching my show.

Lana came to sit beside me and mumbled under her breath, "This is *my* house. You can't tell me shit to say or do in my house."

Maybe she thought I couldn't or didn't hear her, but I did. Feeling a tad bit bothered by her sudden need to have a problem with me really worked my nerves. I sat there pretending that everything was fine. I looked at my wineglass, which was halfway empty, and saw my reflection. She whispered to me, "*Show her who runs this*." And I couldn't have agreed with her more. Lana needed to learn her place.

Smashing the wineglass on her wooden coffee table, I took the sharpest piece of it and placed it near her throat. "Don't think I didn't hear you. We are related by blood. I know you never loved me, sister, and that's fine. Once we get those people responsible for Becca's death, I'll be gone forever. But if you keep fucking with me, you'll be with them, floating in the nearest river."

"Dareen!" my sister uttered as I pressed the glass on her throat.

"Do you understand me?" I asked, gripping the glass so tightly it was beginning to cut my hand.

"Yes, Dareen, I got it!" The words escaped through her teeth.

"Great. Now, let's grab some dinner and watch a movie or something." I took the glass out of my hand, placing it on the coffee table.

Lana left the living room, not saying another word to me. I wasn't about to chase after her. She could have her little tantrum, and when she cooled off, we could move on.

Lana

I didn't know what was wrong with my sister. She must have lost her mind, almost stabbing me like that. I knew Dareen had a crazy side to her, and to be honest, I never thought she would ever show it to me directly. There was a reason why I changed my name and tried to stay as distant as possible. When we graduated from high school, I decided that I didn't want to be with my other two siblings because I wanted to find myself and grow.

I remember when Dareen messaged me on Facebook from Rebecca's account. At first, I didn't want to believe her. But when I video-called her through Messenger, the evidence was so compelling that I had no choice. I don't regret her telling me the truth and us being around each other again. I regret allowing her to live here with me. She has little to no respect for me or my home. I worked hard to be a badass psychologist at 25.

I left my crazy other half in the living room and went to run me a bath. I needed to relax from the day I had. Tommy was my last client, and every session with him was emotionally draining for me, so I could only imagine how it was for him. He refused to tell me the information I needed—*we* needed—to get him and his friends convicted. I wanted revenge for my Rebecca. She didn't deserve to be murdered and mutilated the way Dareen described.

Rebecca and I have always remained close throughout the past few years. I made her vow not to tell Dareen about my whereabouts or our relationship. I know it sounds bad that a set of triplets couldn't be close or even best friends. But Dareen always made things between us difficult, from her crazy antics to pure jealousy of us. It was just best for us to cut ties. I would always love her (in my Whitney Houston voice), but even now, I can't wait to get rid of her again.

When this is over, I may even move. Maybe across country so I could be rid of her until she dies or something. I waited 'til my Jacuzzi was filled almost to the top before cutting off the water. Then I pulled my twenty-four-inch body wave Brazilian hair into a high ponytail, slipped out of my clothing, and got into my piping-hot bath. The scent of the strawberry bubble bath filled the bathroom.

As I soaked in the tub, I played my '90s R&B playlist to help mellow my mood. As the music took my mind off my day, I closed my eyes, feeling a sense of tranquility. As I reclined in the tub, a cold shiver ran over me, but I shook it off and closed my eyes, trying to erase the last thirty minutes from my mind.

Just as I closed my eyes, Rebecca's face appeared to me. She had this heavenly glow surrounding her. I didn't know if I was dreaming or if this was actually happening. I reached out to touch her, and my hand went straight through like she was a ghost. I told her how much I missed her, and she just smiled. After blowing me a simple kiss, she disappeared right before my eyes.

I splashed water on my face, then looked around for my dear sister. But Rebecca was nowhere to be found. I got out of the tub, grabbing my purple Egyptian cotton bath towel to wrap around me as I walked back into my bedroom. My heart felt as if it had sunk to the pit of my stomach.

Lying on my bed to air-dry, all I wanted was another chance to see her. I went through my phone and looked through my picture gallery. Seeing all of the pictures we took the week before her untimely death made my heart break worse than any breakup or anything that ever happened to me in my life. I cradled my phone into my chest as I whispered, "*I will avenge and get the truth for you. I love you, Becca.*"

CHAPTER THREE

Tommy

The following Monday, I decided to return to work. It had been awhile since I had seen the inside of my office. I once enjoyed going there. The strain on Eric's and my friendship since he murdered my love has made things difficult.

I got to the office around ten that morning, and everyone seemed elated to have me back, but I wasn't as excited. I took my time going through the office. My assistant was at her desk, already getting things done. When she saw me, she also welcomed me back.

Before heading into my office, I noticed Eric's office door was wide open. So, I decided to go over to speak. Now, as he was my best friend, he tried hooking me up with countless girls over the year, and it just didn't feel right. I hoped that when I went to talk to him, he wouldn't try another blind date.

I knocked on his door to gain his attention. "Aye, bro, you busy?" I asked him, peeking in.

Eric looked up with a smile when he heard my voice. "Hey, Tommy. What's going on?"

I stood in the doorway of his office and said, "Eric, we need to talk."

"Well then, why the hell are you just standing there? Come on in, bro," he said, seeming happy to see me and even more excited to talk to me.

I walked into his office, shutting the glass door behind me. With everything that had happened, I tried to keep our brotherhood alive, but it was extremely difficult for me because I blamed him for everything. No matter how they tried to paint Monica, aka Dareen, as this evil, crazy, vindictive bitch, I couldn't see her that way. There were two sides to Dareen, and I got to experience the good, fun-loving side.

"What's up? How are things going with that girl, Lisa, I set you up with?" he asked as I sat in his crimson-colored armchair.

"I couldn't trust her. I don't trust any woman right now, really. Who's to say they aren't another Dareen?" I looked around his office at all the pictures of his family and us hanging on the walls.

"Wait," Eric said, laughing. "You couldn't trust her? Tommy, you've only been seeing her for a week or so. You didn't give it enough time."

"Well, you know my guard is up, wondering if anything is real. Don't want another situation like last year." I hung my head as I thought of Dareen.

"Yeah, man, I guess. What's really on your mind? I can tell that's not what you wanted to talk about," he said, turning to lift his window behind his desk to smoke a cigar.

Eric offered me one of his Cubans. I took it, and as I got ready to light it, I could see Dareen's reflection through the window. I leaned back in the chair, taking a deep breath before placing the cigar to my lips. With Eric's back turned to me, I blurted out that I had been seeing Dareen in my dreams.

"Tom, you serious right now?" Eric looked shocked to hear that I was dreaming of her.

"Yeah. I see her sometimes when I'm awake. Like she's haunting me for not fighting for her. I've been seeing a therapist too," I mentioned as I took another puff from the cigar.

"Tommy, I . . . I didn't think or know things were like this. You seeing a shrink? What have you told them?" Eric seemed more concerned about what information was told to my therapist than my own mental state.

"I haven't mentioned anything if that's what you're more concerned about, bro. I'm seeing her so I can try to sleep and live a normal life again. I wasn't fucked up till she came into my life, and y'all killed her," I shouted at him, fuming with anger.

"Tommy, this *isn't* our fault. It isn't *your* fault. Dareen was a cancer that had to be killed, or she would've killed us. Why can't you get that?" Eric screamed back at me in frustration.

"Yeah, I hear you," I mumbled as I turned my head to face the other direction.

Eric lit his cigar and took his first hit before calmly saying to me, "Man, bro, it's going to be all right. Why didn't you tell us?"

I chuckled at the fact that he wanted me to confide in him. "Shit hasn't been the same. You know that shit, man. So, why would I tell you?"

"You just need to let it all go, especially her. You can always talk to me. We are family, and that's stronger than any friendship. Don't you forget that," Eric stated as he leaned back in his coffee-colored, reclining desk chair.

"Eric, you never told me a lot of things that I still have questions about," I expressed, hoping that he would tell me more about their history.

"Told you what?" he asked.

"About why Dareen wanted to be Monica? Why she came after me? You have to know why she played with me like that," I insisted.

"Nigga, how the fuck was I supposed to know?" Eric got hostile as I pressed more about Dareen.

"You should've known *something* was up. I showed you pictures. You could have prevented this," I yelled, slamming my hand on the arm of the chair.

"Tommy, I never saw an actual picture of her. The one time you were going to show me, I had to go. I never saw her till that night. You *know* that. So, chill with that shit, man," he said as he got out of his chair, staring straight at me like he wanted to fight.

"Still, bro," I stated, not feeding into his anger.

Eric leaned over his desk, shouting, "Still *what?* That bitch was the fucking devil!"

"Don't disrespect her, and she is *not* the devil." I stood up, slamming my fist into his desk. If he kept talking that way, I knew this conversation was going to turn into an altercation.

"She ain't *what,* Tommy? You slamming shit on my desk like you gonna do something?" Eric came around to face me.

"Eric, *don't* play with me. I will beat your ass in here, boys or not. You gonna respect that woman—dead or not." I shoved him out of my face.

"She wasn't *what?* A danger? A nutcase? A fucking lunatic? She tried to *kill* my wife twice and kidnapped my child, *your* goddaughter. Yet, here you are, *still* trying to defend her." Eric shoved me twice while he scolded me like a child.

"She was scared. If that was your daughter, what would you have wanted to happen to her?" I said it, trying to imply guilt so Eric could see where I was coming from, but it was like hitting a brick wall.

"*Seriously,* Tommy? How you know she was scared? You still stuck up her ass, huh? She played you and used you to get what she thought she wanted. And she *still* lost. My daughter would *never* do no bullshit like that!" Eric pushed me so hard I almost lost my balance.

"Eric, you got one more time to push me like that—and you're wrong," I hollered.

"No, Tommy, you *know* I'm right. I hate to say it like that. But look at you. The past year, you been walking around like a drunk zombie. Get it together, man." Eric backed away from me, folding his arms.

I said nothing as I stood by the wall. Eric continued to ramble on and on about letting the past go and moving on. But he honestly knew how that shit felt for me. His wife is still here. The woman I wanted to marry wasn't.

"Yo, as my brother, I'm telling you to stay home. You don't have to be in the office to get work done. If you can't make it to a meeting, I'll fill you in. But I need *Tommy* back. So if you need more time, then take it, man," Eric suggested, but I wasn't trying to take off more time to deal with this pain.

I said nothing in response to him. I just gathered myself and tried to be as calm as possible, stepping back. Once I departed from his office, I headed back across the hall to my office. I provided my assistant with instructions on ways to reach me from home since I would be working from there. I also asked her to keep me updated on any changes within the office.

Looking around my office, I gathered what I could and headed to my car. Walking to the garage, I could see Dareen clear as day, as if she were right there beside me. Her presence lingered near me, and it felt so real. I got to my car, and as I blinked my eyes, her chopped-up body image was facing me. I blinked again, and there she was, asking me why I didn't save her.

I was so unaware of my surroundings. I ran out into the middle of the garage, trying to escape the images haunting me.

"Tommy! Tommy!" Reneece yelled, getting out of her car, breaking me out of my trance. "Are you all right? Why were you just standing in the road like that?" she asked.

"Yeah, yeah, I'm fine. I thought I saw something." I peeked over at my car, and the bloody image was finally gone.

Reneece had her hands on my shoulders, looking around, trying to see if she could figure out what spooked me. "You were screaming Dareen's name over and over," she said, looking at me with a face full of concern.

"No, no, I wasn't. You're hearing things, sis," I said, playing it off, but I knew she wasn't lying.

"Tommy, yes, you did. I heard you. You *sure* you, okay?" she asked again.

"Reneece, I *said* I was okay. Can you drop it?" I stated sternly.

"Okay. I was just making sure," she whispered as she let go of my shoulders.

"Reneece, I'm good, I promise. Sorry for yelling." I apologized to her for being an asshole. I knew she was only trying to be there for me.

Reneece backed up, looking at me with concern. "We are family always. I love you; we all love you," she stated.

She gave me a sisterly hug and kiss before telling me to drive safely. I watched her get back into her car and park farther down in the parking lot. Once she was out of my view, I got into my vehicle. Looking in my rearview mirror, there she was again. She was telling me I was worthless, and I would never be whole again. She told me her death was my fault. It was fucking with my mind.

I let out a scream, hoping it would make her go away. Then I sped off with no destination in mind. I'm starting to believe her. There was more I should have and could have done. But I didn't.

Eric

I was speaking with Tommy's and my assistants, providing them with a game plan to make all of our jobs easier since Tommy wouldn't be working so much for a while. As I was talking to them, I felt someone grab me from behind. Before snapping at the person, I saw that it was Reneece. I left the group meeting to talk to my wife.

"Babe, I got you," Reneece teased as she let go of my waist.

"Yeah. I should've been paying better attention. You almost got elbowed," I joked with her before kissing her cheek.

"Well, that's good. Can't nobody hug you from behind like that but me," she said, chuckling, and then continued to say, "I saw Tommy in the garage."

I guided her toward my office and told her, "Yeah, he decided to work from home for a while."

"Is that why he was lookin' all crazy and callin' Dareen's name?" Reneece asked me as she entered my office.

"What? What are you talkin' about?" I questioned. I was trying to understand what she was telling me because it made no sense to me.

"I almost ran over him because he was calling her name and walking in the middle of the road. He was like out of it. He just kept saying 'Dareen' over and over, while he was walking. Like he was talking to her or something," Reneece disclosed to me.

"It's worse than I thought. I guess that's why he said he's been seeing a shrink," I babbled out, not realizing Reneece heard me.

"What? For how long?" Reneece's eyes bulged out in shock.

"I'm not sure," I said as I came from behind my desk. "He came in here earlier, goin' off 'bout that bitch Dareen, I just thought he needed more time to get it out of his system, but maybe something deeper is going on."

"Tommy fell in love with her. Maybe he's haunted by their love. Or the fact that he wanted a future with her that will never be now," Reneece said as she moved her chair closer to mine.

"You know, I can see that. Aye, remember that one episode in *Power,* the one where Tommy killed off Holly? *That's* how he's acting," I stated, laughing out loud as I thought back to that episode when he killed Holly and started sniffing more coke. I just prayed that my Tommy wasn't going off that badly.

"Eric, that's not funny." Reneece shook her head at me in disappointment.

"I know, babe, just trying to lighten things up a bit," I chuckled, but quickly stopped when Reneece wasn't laughing with me.

"Listen, he's your best friend, our brother. We have to look out for him. We have no idea what he's really going through," Reneece said.

"You're right, babe. Maybe I'm going too hard on him." I realized that maybe Tommy needed more love than the backlash.

"Well, all we can do as friends is be there. We have to be there for him, no judgments, no attitudes, and no blaming. He's truly hurting, and we need to be his backbone right now. Give him the strength he can't seem to find within himself right now." Reneece held my hands as she tried to reason with me about Tommy, and maybe she had a point.

"That's why I love you." I kissed her and said, "Make sure the door is locked. I want you."

"You want me?" Reneece bit her bottom lip, enticing me as she looked deep into my eyes.

"Mmm-hmm, right on this desk." I moved my office supplies to the side, making space for me to have my way with her.

"Oh, really?" Reneece winked at me before obeying my instructions.

Rising from the chair, moving to my office door, locking it, and closing the blinds, she secured our privacy. I took that time to start unbuttoning my purple silk dress shirt. She turned back around and walked to me seductively. When she met me standing in the middle of my office, she dropped to her knees while loosening my belt.

Reneece wasted no time getting down to business. My eyes rolled in the back of my head as I muttered, "Fuck." Just from the first few moments of sucking on me, she was making a nigga ready to knock her up again. I moved her hair out of her face so I could watch her suck me like a Blow Pop. She looked so beautiful with my dick in her mouth. I enjoyed the view.

Reneece played with her kitty as she continued sucking my dick. I don't know what got into her today, but she was sucking my dick like she was never going to see me again. Her throat muscles relaxed, allowing me to slide my dick down her throat. I saw her rubbing her pussy as she topped me off. She was moaning so much that I started to feel like she was enjoying this more than I was.

I pushed her back gently, taking my hardened dick out of her mouth. Guiding Reneece to the corner of my desk, I sat her on top of it and slid her leopard print panties down to the floor before kneeling. Then I placed my head between her thighs. I loved the way she smelled and tasted. I couldn't wait to put her on the tip of my tongue.

I sucked on her clit as I moved my hands toward her breasts to caress her nipples. She gripped my head as her juices flowed on my tongue. I could feel her pussy throbbing as I slipped my left index finger inside her. Standing up, I continued to massage her tight, pink pussy with my finger and could tell she was ready to explode again.

I take great pleasure in pleasing my wife. Every taste and touch of her gives me life. I didn't want her to come on my finger. I wanted to feel those juices on my dick. I took my finger out, letting her taste her own juices. I licked my lips before asking her if she liked how it tasted. She nodded her head while smiling at me with her eyes. Spreading her beautiful, thick thighs, I slid inside her.

Her nails dug into my arms as she let out a slight gasp. I stroked inside her treasure slowly, easing every inch of me into her. The wetness of her pink sea that surrounded my dick felt so good to me.

Every time we made love, it was amazing. Even after everything we've been through, our love seemed to grow stronger with every trial. I loved looking at my wife's facial expressions while I made love to her. The more she moaned, and even when we would lock eyes, it made me go harder. I sped up my strokes, instructing her to look into my eyes. I pumped my dick into her harder and deeper until I felt my head hit her G-spot. I had to place her panties into her mouth when her moans got louder. Moments later, I felt her body shivering from her climax as her pussy squirted all over my dick and desk.

After I exploded inside of her, I lay there on top of her. Reneece kept her arms around my waist as we caught our breath. I was easing my way out of her pussy that was still dripping wet when someone knocked on the door. After

I told whoever it was that I would be out in a few, they walked away without saying a word.

"Back to work it seems, my darling husband," Reneece teased as she caressed my dick softly.

"That work isn't as fun as working on you," I said, kissing my wife and not wanting to get back to business.

As we were getting up, my phone started ringing. I ignored it the first time, but whoever it was kept calling back-to-back. Reneece pushed away from me gently and told me to answer the phone.

I answered, but kept my hands on Reneece's pussy.

"Hello?"

"Hey, is this Eric?" a male voice asked from the other end of the phone.

"Yes. How can I help you?" I responded while keeping my wife's perfect, naked body in my eyesight.

"This is Jesus, the main electrician. We need you to get here right away," he stated with a sense of urgency in his voice.

"Well, I'm at lunch with my wife right now. Can you talk to Tommy about what's going on?" I asked, trying to get him off my phone. The more Reneece sat in my view, the harder my dick got again.

"Eric, man, you've got to get down here right away. Tommy is on the roof, just sitting here. He looks bad and smells like he's been drinking," my electrician told me, sounding nervous.

Reneece and I looked at each other. Before I took Jesus off speakerphone, I said, "I'll be right there. Call the police."

"Eric, baby . . ." Reneece mumbled, sounding shocked but also scared for our friend.

"We have to hurry. Tommy needs us. He needs help. I can't let him do this," I told her as I kissed her forehead before moving to the other side of the office, searching for our clothing.

Dressing quickly, we ran out of the office. I stopped at the main receptionist desk since my secretary was gone for lunch. I provided detailed instructions on who should leave messages on our desk lines and who should call my cell while I was out.

We made our way to the parking garage. I told Reneece we would take her car for now. While getting in the car, I knew that if Tommy wouldn't listen to us, he would surely listen to his sister, Ashley. She had texted Reneece the other day, saying she would be in town for a Delta Airlines conference. Reneece had beat me to the punch when she told me she sent Ashley an SOS text about Tommy and provided her the location to meet us at. She responded quickly, saying she was still at least two hours away. So, we were on our own to save him.

I sped toward our construction site, praying I would reach my friend in time. I could only hope to save him from making a terrible mistake. Approaching the site, my heart fluttered with nervousness. My mind wandered. I began questioning myself. *Was I being a supportive friend? Did I do all I could to help Tommy heal?*

CHAPTER FOUR

Tommy

I was sitting on the rooftop edge, where our construction team was finishing a new office building for a client. I was a mess. I was blubbering through my tears while talking to Dareen as her spirit came to me. Her body was bruised and mangled. I couldn't take seeing her that way.

I looked at the spirit haunting me, yelling out, "Why did you do this to me? You lied, you used me, and look what you made me do. Look what you made them do."

Dareen shook her head and said, "Eric made you do this to me. Made you help them. I never wanted anything but just to be happy."

Hanging my head low, I whispered, "But not with me," while more tears fell from my eyes.

"Yes, with you. Tommy, don't you see it was all a plan? They got in the way of our happiness," Dareen scolded me, and she was right.

Her spirit was tormenting me, but she was right. I didn't fight for us as I should have. Hearing her voice was driving me insane. I didn't know what was real or not anymore. "Bitch, leave me alone. Get the fuck out of my head and just leave me alone," I shouted as I hit my head, trying to erase her image from my brain.

While I was trying to clear my mind, I heard Reneece approach me cautiously. "Tommy, Tommy, can you hear me?"

"Yes, I hear you." I turned around slowly to face her.

"Why don't you come off that ledge? Eric and I are here, and we want to help. Whatever it is, whatever is wrong, we can fix it together, okay? Come on, bro, come back inside." Reneece motioned for me to come near her.

She was walking toward me to meet me halfway when I noticed Eric coming up behind her. Looking at my so-called brother, I realized this was all his fault, and I snapped. I pushed Reneece out of my way and sprang toward Eric.

"Tommy, the fuck is wrong with you? I'm *not* going to fight you," Eric yelled, trying to avoid me.

"This is all *your* fault. You may not fight me, but I'm gonna beat your ass, my nigga," I spat and threw a right hook at him, but missed.

Reneece tried to break us up, but I was too far into my feelings to let it go. I could hear others trying to intervene, but my eyes were locked on Eric. Without realizing it, Reneece got caught in my wrath. I was attempting to land a punch on Eric's jaw when I hit her instead. Reneece got my hardest punch ever and fell to the ground, hitting her head on one of the boulders that were stacked adjacent to where we were standing.

Eric stopped to rush to her side. Reneece wasn't responding to him, and when he touched the back of her head, traces of her blood dripped from his fingertips.

"Eric, I'm sorry. I wasn't-I wasn't thinking or paying attention." I went closer, trying to help him with Reneece.

"Someone call 911!" Eric shouted as Reneece lay in his arms. "Tommy, get the fuck away from us."

"Eric, my brother, I wasn't paying attention." I moved away to give him some space.

"Man, just leave me alone 'cause I don't wanna say the wrong shit to you right now—or worse." Disappointment and anger filled my friend's eyes.

"I just wanna make sure she's all right. You want me to go to the hospital with you?" I questioned. I wanted to be there for both of them.

Eric looked over to see the paramedics and police rushing in, then said to me, "Man, just move out of the way. If I need you for something other than business, I'll call."

The paramedics came in and took Reneece out of the building within moments. A police officer pulled Eric aside and questioned him. I for sure thought he would try to press charges against me. I would not blame him if he did. I stood near the door as Eric followed behind the officer. As they were leaving, I reached out, patting him on the back.

Brushing my hand away, Eric shouted, "You are *dead* to me. I don't give a fuck how you feeling 'bout that stupid-ass bitch Dareen. *No one* harms my wife! That includes *you,* my nigga."

I wanted to go after him, but I realized that we all just needed some time and space. I had made a complete spectacle of myself and realized that everyone now thought I was going crazy. I headed out of the construction site, not knowing where to turn.

Later that day . . .

I drove around for a few hours, unsure where to go. Eventually, I stopped at a liquor store and bought $200 of liquor. Within an hour, a bottle and a half were already gone. Somehow, I ended up at Dr. Lana Morane's office.

I stumbled into her office, wasted, passed her secretary, and banged on her office door until she let me in. She was shocked to see me there.

"Tommy, what are you doing here? Are you drunk?" she asked, blocking the doorway.

I bum-rushed her, letting myself into the office. "Doc, I need to see you. I need to talk to you, *please*."

"Tommy, what's wrong?" I heard her close the door slowly behind me as I made myself comfortable in her black velvet chair.

"I'm seeing her everywhere. I can't get her out of my mind. I attacked my best friend, and his wife is in the hospital because of me. I can still hear her voice even if I can't see her. She's *always* here." Placing my hands over my eyes, I let out a subtle scream.

She pulled her desk chair out to sit near me. "Who's always here? Who are we talking about, Tommy?"

"Monica, Dareen, whoever the fuck she was. She won't leave me alone. I can't get rid of her." I felt like I was losing my mind.

"Tommy, take a deep breath for me." She passed me a water bottle before getting one for herself.

"Tommy, talk to me. Tell me who this person is who is haunting you." She paused and looked at me. "Do you mind if I record this session?" she asked, pulling out a small, black rectangular box.

"What the fuck do you mean record?" I asked, baffled about why she would try that with me, of all people.

"Tommy, look, it's really just something that a lot of therapists do." She tried to enlighten me on their so-called procedures.

"Nah. You got me fucked up. Yes, I fucking mind. I may be going through some shit that you may not fucking understand. My name is everywhere. You wanna tarnish it, is that it? You trying to make a joke out of me?" I asked her as my frustration built. With a heavy breath, I exhaled and said, "This was all a mistake. I thought you wanted to help me. But none of y'all help. You're just some trick-ass bitch making money without spreading her fucking legs." I was pissed that she asked me that shit. I even wondered how often she may have recorded our conversations without me knowing.

Dr. Lana put the recorder away as she said to me, "Listen to me. I get that you are going through something major, and I may have upset you and thrown you off about the recording. But *don't* disrespect me," she said sternly, cutting her eyes at me.

I got frustrated with her. "*You* disrespected *me* by trying to record me to tarnish me."

"Tommy, I wasn't, nor would I ever, want to do that. Sometimes, with my patients' consent, I record so I can take notes after our sessions and try to figure out some ways I can help that we can go over during the next visit," she went on to explain.

"Yeah, whatever." I rolled my eyes, realizing that I probably should have just come at a different time.

"Tommy, listen, please, sit down." She tapped the chair for me to sit back and listen to her a bit longer.

"Look, I know that I'm just crazy, and I'm OK with coming to terms with that. I just gotta deal with this shit right now," I exclaimed, punching the arm of my chair.

"Tommy, I care about you. I care about you as a person. You don't have to be crazy or anything like that to talk to me. Sometimes, you need a listening ear, a friend," she said.

I slapped my hand across my right knee, bursting into laughter before I said to her, "Listen, ma'am, no disrespect, but you still tryin'a get a check up out of me. A friend, shorty? A friend? You're my *friend?*"

"Tommy, I want to be anything I can be to you. I only wanna be there for you. I can be your friend *and* your therapist. You have to trust me." Dr. Lana finished writing in her black leather notebook before taking a look at me.

I laughed in her face, making the doctor feel as if her attempts were going nowhere. "Yeah, you my friend all right, with a $500 bill for spending time with my friend. May as well be a prostitute."

"Tommy, I want to help." She placed her notebook on the table, uncrossing her legs to lean forward in front of me.

"No, you wanna be paid. Which I am already paying you enough for," I sniggered sarcastically.

"Tommy, please, just let me in. Let me be here for you," she begged, reaching her arm out toward me.

"Goodbye, Doc. Thanks for what you did or didn't do so far." I had had enough for the day and decided to leave.

Before I could go, she grabbed my wrist, guiding me back to my seat. Dr. Lana asked me to stay in a sweet, soft voice. Then she kissed me. I wanted to stop her, but for a quick second, she looked like my Monica, and I went in with tongue action and all. When I opened my eyes and looked again, I realized she wasn't Monica, aka Dareen. Snapping back into reality, I quickly stopped before things went any further.

Dr. Morane easily unzipped the back of her dress, revealing her matching black-and-red lace lingerie set. She had a little tummy, thick chocolate thighs covered in tattoos, and nipples that were hardened poked through her bra. I could see the horniness in her demeanor.

"Look, Dr. Lana, or if you want, Dr. Morane. Like, I really don't know what to say." I shook my head in disbelief.

"Listen, this is way against my business, my oath as a psychologist. But I want you, and I want you inside me. I've been thinking about it for some time," she said to me.

"What? You want me to pour my heart *and* shit out to you? What, you gonna fuck my problems away?" I shouted, feeling offended but yet flattered that I still looked good enough to fuck.

"Tommy, listen," she said, "I want you to release it on me. No talking, no notes, nothing. Let me be everything you need, *and* more."

Dr. Morane unhooked her bra, releasing her triple-D-sized breasts, and dropped to her knees. Against my better judgment, my cock was ready for some action. My mind wandered off, thinking of how her pussy would feel on my dick, which only excited me more.

I pulled away, trying to regain control, but my therapist and my other head had other plans. The way Dr. Lana looked at me so erotically, my cock was ready to jump down her throat. For the first time since we'd been meeting, I took notice of her figure. Her body was so curvaceous and thick. What man wouldn't want to have her in their bed?

Rubbing my dick through my pants, I asked her, "Is this really what you want, Doc?"

"Yes. I want you. I want you *now*." She let out a slight moan with her reply.

"Are you sure?" I questioned, making sure I wasn't overstepping my boundaries.

"Yes, Tommy, give it *all* to me," she pleaded, lying on the floor of her office, spreading her pussy wide open for me to see her pink pearl.

All of my pain, frustration, and anger found its long-awaited target. I quickly threw my shirt on the ground. Her eyes twinkled in delight as they gazed over my swollen, beefed-up arms and chiseled chest with my Kappa Alpha Psi tattoo on my upper right pectoral. I didn't vacillate once. I leaned forward, placing her legs around my neck, and started to eat her out.

She was enjoying how this tongue felt on her clit. Her moans were tantalizing to my ears. She knew how to get her nut, and I was going to let her do her thing. After her breaths got heavy, I knew she was almost there, but I was going to get her. I lifted my head back just as she was coming, so I could see her reaction.

Dr. Lana Morane was about to get some work. She could barely talk as I filled her mouth with my dick. After I got her to taste me in return, I lifted her legs in the air and slid inside her.

"Oh, you tryin'a come on my dick?" I asked in between breaths as I still stroked her pussy.

"Mmm-hmm," she moaned.

"Not yet, you nasty-ass bitch. Bend over," I instructed her as I slapped my dick on her soft, round ass cheeks.

I could tell she liked that shit. She seemed as if her sex life was boring, so I was going to give her all of me. I grabbed her hair with one hand, and the other gripped her waist as she gave me that perfect posture to hit it from behind. My dick slid inside of her pussy. It was so tight and wet. I was already enjoying myself.

Dr. Lana got tired of me being in control and switched things up on me. Pushing me onto her white sheep rug, she fell on my dick in a full split. Her ass cheeks clapped while she touched her toes, preparing to ride me.

My dick filled her insides as she rode me reverse cowgirl style. The way she bounced her ass on me, I knew she was trying to make me come. But she wasn't about to get me like that. I grabbed her hair, pulling her head closer to me. The tighter my hold got, the more she slowed down while grinding on my dick and tightening her pussy muscles on my shaft.

Dr. Morane was reaching her peak. She didn't want to stop, and was she ready for me to release. She begged me not to come yet, but my dick was ready to tap out. It had been a year since I had some bomb-ass sex. I was so backed up, and she was about to get a sea of cum over her body. I picked her up as she wrapped her legs around my waist, penetrating her in the air like some straight porn shit. I wanted to pull out, but her wetness felt so good, I couldn't help myself. I got lost in the sauce and exploded inside her.

I placed her down gently, then grabbed some of the tissues off of the coffee table to clean her cum off my dick. Now, an awkward silence filled the room, and I realized it was time for me to go. Looking around, I searched for my clothes so I could go home.

"Tommy?" Dr. Lana whispered my name while keeping her eyes glued to my naked body.

"Yeah?" I answered, wondering why she was calling my name.

"Maybe we should talk about what happened," she suggested as she searched for her clothing.

"Yeah, but I think all of that spoke for itself," I said, pulling my Gucci boxers back on, trying to dodge any conversation.

"Tommy, I just don't want you to think—" Dr. Lana started, but I cut her off.

"Think that you fuck every man that's a client of yours?" I asked, wondering if she had more male clients that she was fucking on the low.

"I hope you don't think that. I truly like you, and I am attracted to you. I couldn't help it. I've been wanting to do this for a min now," she said to me as she pulled up her dress.

"That's cool, Miss Lady. There's no need to talk. Not now, possibly never again." I could feel the awkwardness in the air.

I finished dressing, grabbed my blazer, and walked out of the office. I said no goodbyes and didn't even look back. I just fucked my therapist. We had crossed that line. Now, I have to figure out whether I can continue seeing her for help or if it would be best to find someone new. But Dr. Lana Morane gave me a sense of safety and peace, something I wasn't sure if I could ever have again.

CHAPTER FIVE

Lana

Tommy had left me in my office feeling like shit. All of this started as part of a master plan, but the more I saw Tommy and his pain, the more I realized he was tremendously hurt. But he threw me off when he said Dareen's name instead of Rebecca's. I was confused because the story my sister told me led me to believe Tommy was with Becca. But was he *really* with Dareen? Why did he think she was dead? I needed to get the real story because shit wasn't adding up.

Even though we were identical triplets, I spent a lot of money I got when I was fucking with this military guy in my undergrad college years to have a great deal of cosmetic work done so that I would no longer look like my sisters. I wanted to be my own person and not be mistaken for them. I hated that growing up. One of us would get in trouble, and since they couldn't tell which one of us was the culprit, we all got punished.

I got my skin bleached so I could be a little lighter, my nose done, my waist snatched, and I got a boobs job. I was happy with my appearance. I even went through changing my last name to his after he was killed in Iraq. I had made my own reset on life and was enjoying it until now.

I got partially dressed and reached into my top right desk drawer to grab my bottle of red berry Cîroc. I was going to pour some into a glass, but the way I was feeling, I took the bottle straight to the head. As I sat at my desk drinking, my cell beeped. I looked down and saw that Dareen was texting me.

Dareen: Hey, sis, when are you coming home?

Me: Why?

Dareen: Maybe because I left when you did today, and I have no key.

Me: You don't need a key. You're not a permanent resident.

Dareen: I don't want one of your fuck-ass keys. I don't know what's wrong with you. I just hit you with some simple shit, and you coming at me crazy.

Me: I am not. You're taking it that way. But as long as you are somewhere safe, there's no need for me to rush home.

Dareen: You have no clue where I am. I could be looking at you right now. I could be in the garage of your building.

Me: That's fine. You know what? Maybe I should run a psych eval on you. You seem a little off.

Dareen: LMFAO! Bitch, you hella funny. Sis, maybe you should have been a comedian or some shit.

Me: Dareen, did Tommy know you?

Dareen: No . . . I mean, I saw him maybe a few times. We all went to the same campus. I'm pretty sure I ran into him once or twice. Why?

Me: Just asking.

Dareen: Did you see him? What was he talking about? Did he say my name or something?

Me: Does it matter? Like, why would you care what he said if it wasn't about Rebecca?

Dareen: Lol. All right, sis, you got it. Let me know when you head home. Enjoy the rest of your day.

That heffa was fishing for information, but I wasn't giving her anything. As long as I've been seeing Tommy, she has known nothing about what we've been talking about. I never really said anything because it wouldn't help our case. This whole situation was becoming overwhelming, and I didn't want to deal with any of it.

I knew the sooner I got vengeance for Becca, the quicker my life could go back to normal. But there was something about Tommy that drew me to him. I have never been so attracted to a man like I was with him. I wanted to give him the peace that he hasn't had in a long time. His brokenness made him more desirable. Deep down, I was broken about my past and my relationships with my sisters. I wanted to vent to him sometimes so he could see that he was safe with me.

I swallowed the last drop of the bottle before walking over to my trash can to throw it away. As I approached it, I looked up, noticing the picture hanging above it of Rebecca's and my graduation night. That night was such a blast. I don't think I had ever been that drunk before.

We both graduated on May 12th around the same time, so we couldn't be at each other's ceremony. So, we decided we would celebrate later. She met me at my apartment around six that evening. I was in the kitchen cooking up some fried lamb chops, rice, mac and cheese, and black-eyed peas when my doorbell rang. I turned the fire on low so nothing would burn. Then I opened my door, and there she was, glowing like the North Star, her diploma in hand, with her NCCU alumni crop top, burgundy tights, and black boots.

"Ayyyyeeee, bitch! I see another graduate in the house," I screamed with excitement as we embraced.

"Twerk, twerk, twerk, twerk that ass," Rebecca giggled after kissing my left cheek.

"Come on in, girl. Help yourself to whatever. Let me finish this food," I instructed, walking backward in my hallway.

"Shit, you know *I will," Rebecca laughed out loud. "It smells so good in here. Okay, Chef, I'm ready to eat." She teased me while creeping up behind me in the kitchen.*

After we ate dinner and hung out at my house for a bit, we went shopping for some bomb-ass outfits for the graduation party we were going to hosted by this group named Kiss ENT. Now, Kiss did throw the best parties in NC, and it was always fun and mostly drama-free. Considering it would be the last party as a college student, we wanted to go out with a bang.

After spending two hours inside Crabtree Mall, we came out with some hot shit. Everyone would be turning their heads in amazement or jealousy. We had just finished getting dressed when Rebecca wanted to take pictures before we headed to the club.

Becca wore this strapless purple-and-silver sequin dress with cutouts in the back. That dress was beautiful on her and hugged her ass perfectly. She knew how to beat a face too, hunty. Her makeup made the dress pop even more. Her purple and silver glitter eye shadow and her highlights were done so perfectly that her face just glowed.

"Bitch, all your ass and titties out," I said as she twirled in front of me.

"Well, I look good. Shit, you look bomb-ass fuck too, with all that ass out." Rebecca stuck her tongue out at me.

I turned my body sideways, looking in my full-length mirror. "You sure? I don't look fat or anything?"

"Bitch, you look fabulous, sis. Let's take a picture before we go and *another shot." Rebecca grabbed her iPhone and set it on top of my dresser.*

After taking two shots of Patrón apiece, she set the timer on her phone to take our picture. After three takes, we finally got the perfect picture.

I took the picture off my office wall, cradling it to my chest. As my heart yearned for my favorite triplet, I mourned her. I let the tears flow until I passed out on my chaise.

Dareen

After I finished texting Lana, I followed Eric's car to Duke Hospital. All I knew was Reneece was on a stretcher, and I prayed she was dead. It seemed that my dirty work may have been done for me. I took Rebecca's royal-blue 2016 Toyota Camry for myself after her passing so I could get around.

I crept into the hospital, but I didn't see Eric. The receptionist in the ER waiting room had his Beats by Dre headphones on, not paying any attention to me or the waiting room. None of Reneece or Eric's people were inside the waiting room, so I assumed they hadn't arrived yet or were possibly in the back with them. After tapping on the glass between the receptionist and me five times, he finally removed his headphones to help me.

"I'm sorry about that, ma'am. How can I help you?" he asked, looking at me with those hazel-green eyes.

"First, your eyes are so beautiful. Second, I got a call that my sister Reneece was sent here for some kind of accident. Her husband is already here," I stated with a crack in my voice.

"Okay. What's your sister's last name?" he asked, focusing on the computer screen.

"Her name is Reneece Walsh. Her husband is Eric Walsh. Please, I need to know she's okay," I said with urgency.

"She's on the fourth floor in the maternity ward. Her husband has requested that no visitors be allowed at this time. I can call the nurse to see if you can come up," he informed me.

I didn't know what to do at this point. I was stuck between a rock and a hard place. I gracefully declined his offer, stating I would call Eric myself. Walking out of the hospital, I tried to call my sister, but she didn't answer. When Lana didn't answer, I figured she wasn't home yet, so I decided to make a little pit stop at another friend's.

The sun had set, the temperature had dropped, and it was the perfect time to visit my dear friend, Tommy. Occasionally, I got a glimpse of the notes my sister would take home from his file. I wanted to know what his state of mind was. Learning that he was seeing me in his sleep made it easy to fuck with him a little bit. I wanted to drive him crazy enough to rat on his friends—or worse, turn on them. If he could get on Lana's and my side, we would win so easily.

I pulled up to Tommy's dimly lit home and parked on the side of his house, then put on my makeup so I could look like a corpse. This was going to be fun to see his reaction. I just needed to make sure that this would go smoothly. No one needed to know I was still alive, for now, at least.

I finished my makeup and eased my way inside his home with the spare key I had made a few weeks ago. I walked inside, quietly shutting the door behind me, but there was no sign of Tommy anywhere. While walking through his home, I started hearing noises outside. Quickly, I hid inside the broom closet adjacent to the half bathroom.

I could hear someone entering the home. I wasn't sure who it was 'cause they said nothing. From the bottom crack of the door, I could see that the lights were on now. I tried not to make a sound until I knew it was safe to come out. Hearing footsteps getting closer and closer to the closet, I started to hear mumbling from whoever it was, and then they fell into the closet door.

"Fuck, man. I wasted my drink," I heard the familiar drunken voice shout.

"Is that Tommy?" I whispered to myself, putting my ear closer to the door to hear if there were other people with him.

The sounds moved away after grunting to get himself up. I waited about ten minutes before exiting the closet. The lights had been dimmed, and I could hear "Outta My System" by Bow Wow playing from one of the rooms. I tiptoed to the back of the house.

I saw Tommy lying in bed wearing nothing but his boxers. His bottle of Hennessy was lying beside him. As the songs switched to Kevin Gates's "Twilight Breaking Dawn," Tommy started screaming at the top of his lungs. His eyes were closed as he belted out the lyrics. Knowing he would assume this was a dream he would enjoy, and I would too, I slid on top of his pelvis area and grinded my hips on him like I was riding his dick. I lifted my dress, sliding my freshly shaved pussy on his hard, thick dick. It had been a minute since I felt a real thick, big, black dick inside of me. I tossed my pussy up and down on his shaft slowly. Tommy's lips separated as sweet, manly moans emanated from his lips.

I bounced on his dick, fucking him froggy style until I reached my peak. My climax was intense and quick. As the juices from my pussy overflowed on his still-erect cock, I slowly slid off it, hiding by the edge of the bed. I wondered if he thought he was dreaming. Tommy's eyes opened and glanced around his bedroom with his dick in his right hand.

I watched him finish himself off. He jacked his dick so hard and fast that when he came, his whole body jerked. His cum oozed over his legs and ball sack. It was such a thick load of cum. He seemed backed up. After his last grunt, he closed his eyes, took another shot of Henny, and went back to sleep.

Even though the nut was good, my job was not yet complete. If that bitch Reneece wasn't dead, then I wanted Tommy to kill her for me. Crawling over to the edge of the bed where his head was, I stood up, towering over his drunken body. I tapped him once, but he just groaned. I hit him harder the second time. Tommy jumped, sitting straight up in the bed. When he saw me standing there, he scurried to the other side of it.

"Hello, Tommy." I flashed him a smile.

"You're . . . You're here? Is this real? Am I dreaming? Did I die?" Tommy asked, looking around the room and checking his pulse.

"Of course, I'm real. I'll always be real to you, Tommy. You could've saved me, but didn't. Why didn't you? Huh, Tommy? I thought you loved me," I derided as I stepped closer to him.

"Bitch, I fucking loved you and tried to save you several times. And you question *me?* You took me through hell. Look at me now. I can't even function. I see you every-fucking-where. Don't you get it?" Tommy yelled while grabbing me by the throat.

I clawed at his hands until he set me free from his grasp. Then I hung my head as if it were broken, showing the fake cut on my neck. Tommy pulled the covers over him as I asked, "Are you afraid, Tommy?"

"Monica, please, just leave me alone," he begged as he hid under his black cotton sheets like a coward.

"My name is *Dareen*. Don't you *ever* forget that," I shouted, while yanking the sheets from him.

"Dareen, please, I just want to move on. You should move on. You don't have any unfinished business. You should be in heaven with our dead baby." Tommy started to sob without even taking a look at me.

"If that's what you want, Tommy, I'll make you a deal. I'll go away if you finish what I started. Kill Reneece. All of this goes back to her. *She's* the reason why you're like this. She's the reason why *I'm* dead. Don't you understand that? Reneece is the problem." I tried to get Tommy to side with me.

"No, *your* choices are the reason why you're dead. If I could change it, I would, but I can't. Just please, let us go. Let me go. Please, I'm begging you." Tommy pleaded with me to reason with him, but I wasn't hearing it.

"No! You *all* will pay—unless you decide to kill her. All of you will pay for what you've done to me." I released a sinister laugh into the atmosphere as I backed up toward the bedroom door and was stopped by some solid object that poked my back.

I took the baseball bat hidden behind the bedroom door and walked over to where Tommy was sitting on the bed. I smashed his head with the bat as hard as I could, knocking him out. Then tossing the bat back by the bedroom door, I scurried out before he would awake. Hopefully, that knocked some sense into his head.

CHAPTER SIX

Eric

I was still in shock that Tommy had put my wife in the hospital. When we arrived, the nurses immediately drew blood, which confirmed she was pregnant. Although I was happy with the news, I couldn't really celebrate because Reneece was still out cold. But God was definitely on our side. She suffered a concussion, but the baby was still receiving the oxygen and blood flow it needed to survive. I requested that she have no visitors but me until I spoke with her family and Tommy.

Three days had passed, and Reneece was finally making some progress in her recovery. She started moving her hands and fingers a bit. I brought our daughter Hailey to see her. Taking her finger paintings from day care, I posted them all in her hospital room, along with the flowers sent by all our friends, including Tommy.

While sitting next to my wife's bedside, I received a text from Joe. I had secluded myself from everyone, only going to work, home, and then back to the hospital. From the text, I could tell he wanted something.

Joe: What up, fam? How's wifey doing? You know me and Jalisa be praying for her, ya know. Keep her blessed up.

Me: I appreciate it, brother. Just praying and waiting for her to wake up.

Joe: She will. She will, my brother. You at the hospital now?

Me: Yeah. I may as well live here. I can't leave her bedside. I gotta know she's OK.

Joe: Bro, why don't we link up lata, ya know? Maybe grab a drink, get out for a bit.

Me: Idk. I don't want to leave her alone.

Joe: Jalisa said she'd stay there while we go.

I started thinking about it. Jalisa wouldn't let anything happen to Reneece, I know that, but I still wasn't sure. However, I could use a drink or two after the week I had.

Joe: Hello, what you wanna do?

I looked at the notification and decided to go. I texted him and told him to meet me at Buffalo Wild Wings near South Point Mall. I would head that way once Jalisa arrived at the hospital.

About an hour later, Jalisa was there. She crept into the room quietly, placing her hand on top of my head.

"Hey, bro. How is she?" Jalisa whispered as she stood back to let me up from my chair.

Embracing her with a friendly hug, I responded, "She's stable. Are you sure you can watch her until I get back?"

"Eric, I may not be her relative by blood, but I *am* her sister. I got her, and I got you. Go unwind, have some fun. If anything happens, I'll call right away." Jalisa handed me my pinstriped black-and-white blazer with a smile.

"Jalisa, thank you." I took my blazer and walked over to the head of the hospital bed to kiss Reneece on the forehead before I left.

I walked out of the hospital, a little amped about having a few drinks with my new friend Joe. Since we met him, he's been a true and genuine friend. It was going to be a nice break from the world.

Tommy

The past few days have been crazy. I woke up in my bed one night after having the craziest dream about

Dareen. Something made me feel as if she was truly still alive somehow. I sat in my house drinking bottle after bottle till everything was down to the last drop.

I was sitting on my bed running the images from the dream through my head, trying to make sense of it all. The bat in my bedroom looked like it had been moved, and I even had a sore lump on the back of my head. Was her ghost physically in my room, or was she really alive? I needed answers, but I didn't know where to start or who to ask. I wanted to reach out to my therapist, but things between us have been so weird since I smashed her on the office floor.

I had no food in the house and was finally ready to eat something. I went into the bathroom to brush my teeth for the first time in two days and threw on some clothes so I could go to the grocery store. While I was rinsing my mouth out with my Crest White Mouthwash, my phone started ringing.

Looking down, I saw it was Joe calling. I really had nothing to say to him or anyone. When the accident happened with Reneece, Joe and Jalisa jumped down my throat. I ignored his call and continued getting dressed. I was grabbing a pair of my Tims when he called again.

"Yeah, hello?" I said, placing the phone on speaker while I put on my shoes.

"What's up, my brotha? Where you at?" Joe asked in between coughs.

"You all right over there? You sound like you're choking," I said, sitting up on the bed.

"Man, this kush blow hard, ya know. But I'm calling to ask if you'd come out with us. Eric said he wanted to see you, talk things out," he said before choking on his blunt again.

"Yeah, I don't know about that." I wasn't sure if I could trust Joe.

"Ya hear me now. We all link up, have a few drinks, and move past the bullshit. We going to Buffalo Wild Wings now." Joe was insistent on my coming out when I wanted to stay locked in my home.

"I'll think 'bout it and call you back." I was trying to end the conversation, but Joe started egging me on.

"I know you should link, rude boy. Our friend needs us, and you acting like a pussy wad 'bout this shit," he yelled as his Jamaican accent came out super heavy.

"Brah, who the fuck you talking to? I really don't need this shit. Y'all have no clue what I am or been going through. You just came along. Who said you was my friend or brother?" I got off the bed, heading toward my door, when I stopped to take a deep breath.

"You may not see us as brothers, but I do. Ya got to get over this bullshit, ya know? Come have a drink with us," he insisted, and I could tell he wasn't going to stop until I gave in.

"I'm going to grab some groceries, so I may swing by," I replied, still hesitant, but I knew he was right.

After we disconnected, I didn't even look in the mirror to see how presentable I was. I made my way out the door to meet my friends, then to Walmart for a few things.

I pulled into the parking lot of Buffalo Wild Wings, and like Joe said, both of their rides were already there. I took a deep breath before getting out of the car, taking a minute to prepare myself before going inside. I haven't seen Eric since the accident, and I wasn't sure how he was feeling, but it would be nice to be back on the same page.

Once inside, I spotted Joe and Eric at a table near the bar, with drinks already on it. Walking over to the table, I felt nervous. I didn't know what to expect from Eric. Joe happened to notice me first and waved me down.

"Glad you were able to make it, bro. Now, we can talk," Joe said, greeting me when I got to the table as he took a sip from his Corona.

"Yeah, I'm glad I made it too. What's up, Eric?" I focused on Eric, waiting for him to acknowledge me.

Eric turned his head toward the flat screen mounted on the edge of the bar. He wouldn't say a word to me, so I sparked a conversation with him instead.

"Eric, I'm so sorry for everything that happened. I never wanted any of this. Please, what can we do, bro? At the end of the day, we are family." I pulled out the wooden chair to sit down and talk to my fellas.

Eric kept his focus on the TV that was replaying the Clippers and Lakers game. Then he said to me, "I haven't been able to tell. What kind of fucking brother are you? Attacking me and my wife over someone who tried to kill us several times? A bitch who never gave two shits about you or Joe?"

"Listen, I know this has to be hard—" I started to say, but Eric wouldn't let me finish my statement before interjecting.

"No, you *don't* know. My wife is pregnant and could've lost our baby because of your recklessness. And the crazy thing is, Reneece did nothing to you to deserve that. You ain't nothing but a bitch-ass nigga. So, tell me, how can we be family?" Eric got up as if he were going to swing at me, but Joe stepped in.

"Listen, listen," Joe said, "Eric, sit down. You both are hurting. And now, we can deal with it as a family or don't fuck with one another anymore."

"Man, he just don't get it, and I'm tired of talking about the same shit," Eric shouted at Joe. Then he redirected his attention to me, firmly clutching his beer bottle in his hand.

"And you, Tommy, keep tryin'a blame us. But you ain't blaming the right person. We ain't got you fucked up in the head—she does. And all 'cause you can't let some dumb-ass broad go."

"I love her, Eric. We are men who are in love. How would you be in my shoes?" I questioned them.

"Yeah, you right. Me and Joe are in love. The difference is that our women love us back. That crazy-ass bitch ain't love *nobody*. Not even you or that demon seed she was carrying." Eric threw the baby out in the conversation, and, honestly, any kid should've been left out of the situation.

"She loved you, and *don't* disrespect my unborn seed. Kids is off-fuckin'-limits." I looked into his eyes, feeling the tension build between us.

"Nigga, is you hearing yourself? *Still* defending her. And that baby wasn't yours. Who knows who the father truly was. Shit, if anyone was to be hurt about that baby Dareen killed off, it should be Joe." Eric turned his back to me, waving down the waitress.

"Listen, Eric, we can keep going back and forth, but the reality is, you have the right to feel how you do, and so do I. But if you and Joe are supposed to be my brothers, then I need y'all's support to get through this. Regardless of what Dareen may have or may not have done, I love her. This shit is fuckin' with me, and that's why I'm in counseling." I calmed my tone and leaned back in the chair.

Eric turned back to face me, then shook my hand. "Fine. We can move forward. We are family, and family fights. But we'll get through it."

"See, that's what I'm talkin' 'bout. Now, can we drink? Shit." Joe busted out laughing while trying to flag down another waitress, since the other one never came.

We sat at the table and talked while we waited for the waitress to finish at her other table. As we conversed about the game and just random nigga shit, my phone dinged with a text message.

Unknown Number: Hi, Tommy. This is not a dream. You thought I was dead, but I'm far from dead. I'm coming for everyone. Tell Eric I said he still looks great.

Me: Who is this? Stop playing on my phone.

Unknown Number: Oh, you think I'm joking? You'll see.

I excused myself from the table to try to call the number the text came from. Someone was trying to fuck with me. Whoever it was, I was going to find out. I called the number twice. The first time, it rang; the second time, a message informed me that it was not in service. Infuriated by the game someone was playing, I went back to the table, slamming my phone on it.

"What's wrong with you?" Eric asked, looking at me, curious.

"I just got this text. Then when I call back, it says the number is disconnected. Which one of y'all did this?" I accused them of setting up the prank call.

Joe and Eric paid me no mind and just laughed like I told a joke. They both started calling me crazy.

"The waitress is coming. Hold on, let's order," Joe pointed out.

The waitress came over and looked straight in my direction. She came over with her notepad. Her body was filled out. She had thick thighs in those tights, and I couldn't help but notice her camel toe. Her pussy looked phat. Looking at her, I knew she was about five foot eight, and her boobs sat up right in her pink and black tank top.

"Hello. I'm Rayna, and I'll be taking care of you the rest of the night. What can I get you fellas?" she asked, her eyes still glued to me.

Joe went first, giving his short order. "Can I get a shot of henny? And let me get some wings with fries, and also let me get three double shots of tequila."

She then turned to Eric and asked him, "And what would you like?"

"Yeah, let me just grab some fries and a Cîroc and cranberry. Let me get another Heineken too." Eric passed the young lady his menu.

"Got it," she said. Then she walked over to me, leaning her big titties in my face. "And what can I get for you, handsome?" she asked seductively.

I glanced over the menu again and placed my order. "Ummm, yeah, Miss Lady, let me get a Corona, two shots of Henny, and the lobster tail."

"Would you like it fried or baked?" she asked, jotting down my order on her pad.

"Fried. Add a side of fries and mac and cheese." I wanted to order the entire menu, but we had just gotten some appetizers, so I was going to stop there.

"Got you, big daddy," she said, turning away with a twist in her hips.

When the waitress walked away, Joe and Eric looked at me strangely. They must have noticed something that I didn't. I was looking around, trying to see if I could figure out why they were looking at me like that.

"What's going on? Y'all see something?" I asked, trying to figure out what was happening.

"Boy, you blind?" Joe said, shaking his head.

"What y'all talking about?" I asked, taking a bite of my cheese sticks.

"Shorty was tryin'a push all up on you," Eric said with a chuckle.

I didn't look like my usual self. I looked like a straight bum. I haven't showered in days, my eyes had bags under them, and my clothes were extra baggy. I wasn't anything to catch right now. I just shook my head in disbelief at what the two of them were saying.

"Tommy, yo, we should have her link up with you. Give you some pussy. Know you ain't had any," Joe said to me while slapping my arm jokingly.

Rayna returned with our tray of drinks. She passed out the drinks, then asked if she could get us anything else. Instead of these fools saying no, they attempted to shoot my shot for me.

"Man, she ain't on my mind. Nothing is but this," I told them while pointing to the message on my phone.

"Listen, we will worry 'bout that if there's any truth to it. I'll have my detective look into the number it came from. If there's anything to it, we go from there," Eric said. "Shorty is on her way back. Give her some play."

The waitress came back with our drinks. She gave Joe and Eric theirs first. Then she walked over to me, set my drinks down, leaned toward me, and asked, "Is there anything else you may need?"

"Miss, our friend is a little shy, but it seems like you might be really into him," Eric said to her.

"I would love to let him into me," she said with a smirk while looking dead into my face before turning to walk away. She then turned back to the table, acting as if they had called her back. She walked over to Tommy, pulled out a pen with a napkin, and wrote down her number.

"Well, if he's so shy, his dick isn't. I get off at two. Call me." She placed the napkin in my pants pocket. While her hand was there, she gently rubbed my dick. "You seem so tense. Let me help ease your mind. I'll make you forget about anything or anyone that's stressing you. You too fine to be so tense. I got you," she whispered before licking her lips.

"I will destroy your pussy. Don't play with me," I whispered in her ear while slowly moving my hand down her back, then grabbing her ass.

She licked her lips. “Sounds like a perfect date to me. Call me at two. Let’s see who destroys who.”

I smirked as she grabbed my dick through my sweats, making it stand straight up. She returned with our food about fifteen minutes later. I watched her ass jiggle in those tights she wore as she went to assist another table. We ate and talked about the text. Eric decided to reach out to his detective friend to see if they could get any files on Dareen and her family.

We finished eating, then Eric and Joe got ready to leave. Eric was ready to get back to his wife, and Joe was so drunk he kept saying how he was going to fuck Jalisa. I wish he had spared us the details. The waitress walked past our table one last time, placing her fingers to her ear, saying, “Call me,” out of those luscious lips.

I took my friends’ advice and shot her a text with my address on my way out. I was going to fuck her little ass up like she was begging for, but first, I needed to go home and shower. I couldn’t fuck no bitch with salty, dirty balls. That wasn’t my steelo. Even though my night was going to be preoccupied, I still couldn’t help that there was a glimmer of hope that I might be able to see my beautiful Dareen again.

CHAPTER SEVEN

Lana

It had been two weeks since Tommy was in my office, which wasn't like him. Every time I called or texted him, he ignored my messages and calls. I knew I was wrong for fucking him, but it was so amazing. It was what we both needed. I didn't want it to mess up the bond we built as client and patient. Tommy needed to trust me, so I could find out why Rebecca was really killed.

I started to understand that Tommy was the key to everything. He could help me uncover the lies Dareen may have told me. The burning question is why he believes she's haunting him when Dareen said he was fucking with Becca. It didn't make sense. Even though I didn't really know Tommy at all, I was more inclined to trust him rather than my own flesh and blood.

I tried to get Tommy out of my mind, but it was so hard. I was sitting with another client, but my mind was distracted. All I could see was her lips moving. By the time our session was over, I had one more client for the day, but I was mentally exhausted. Contemplating whether to cancel at the last minute or to thug out the rest of my day was the decision I had to make.

While I contemplated my next move, I searched for Tommy's file to locate his number. I called his phone at least six times, and each time it was declined. I wondered if he didn't answer because he didn't know it was me. Or maybe he did and didn't want to talk to me. I wrote his address on a sticky note and placed it on top of my briefcase so I wouldn't walk out the door without it.

My final client arrived, and she came in on a thousand. Her name was Lyndelle, and I was seeing her and her husband to help with their marital issues. Today was different because her husband wasn't with her. Lyndelle came in, grabbing the box of tissues, blubbering on about some argument they had.

While she talked, I stood in my office window looking at the scenery, and my mind was going a thousand miles a minute.

"Hello? Dr. Morane, do you hear me? Hello? I'm paying you, and you're not even listening to me." Lyndelle slammed her hand on my coffee table, breaking me from my daze.

"I'm so sorry. I just found out my sister was killed. I definitely apologize. I should have been paying better attention." I apologized, using Rebecca's death as my scapegoat.

"Dr. Morane, I'm sorry to hear about your loss. You weren't paying me any attention since I walked in, and now, I know why." Lyndelle began to gather her belongings.

"Deal with your family. I understand, but you should've rescheduled our appointment before I came. I'll stop by the front and make a new appointment."

"Lyndelle, I'm so sorry about this. I appreciate your understanding. Hey, for the inconvenience, I'll be issuing you a full refund and giving you half off your next session," I said, giving her a little smile.

Stopping at the door, Lyndelle said to me, "Yeah, no worries. I'll see you in a week or two. My condolences."

Lyndelle left me alone in my office with just my thoughts. Walking over to my desk, I closed my blinds just enough to allow only a sliver of sunlight to come through. I stood at the window, reminiscing about how Tommy felt inside my walls. My body craved to feel him once more, even though it would be wrong. Since I had a nine-inch, eight-speed vibrator inside my top right desk drawer, I pulled it out and turned it to the highest speed before placing it between my legs. Just feeling the vibrations made my pussy moist. I cleared off the top of my desk so I could position myself just right. My skirt and Victoria's Secret thong hit the floor. Propping the vibrator in the middle of the table, I climbed on top to ride it.

I was just getting into the groove of things when I heard a bang on the door. Switching off my vibrator but keeping it still inside, I waited for whoever it was to go away. I waited a few moments, but the knocks came again, only louder.

"Hold on, please, I'm just finishing up something," I hollered at the door while getting myself together.

I put it away and quickly dressed, then opened my office door. I was frustrated that I couldn't get my nut, but I wasn't going to keep whoever it was waiting. And there was Dareen, standing there, dressed like a homeless person. She was covered in rags and hung her head as if she was trying not to be seen.

Letting her into my office, I said, "You're supposed to be at home."

"I'm tired of being cooped up in the house. You act like I'm a prisoner and not allowed to leave unless I leave when you do. Like, I'm not a child," she said as she stomped past me.

"But you didn't have to come here. You didn't have to come to my job. So, why did you?" I asked, standing by the door with my arms folded.

Dareen was bent over, going through my mini fridge. "I wanted to see my sister."

"And *my* sister could have waited for me to get home to see me. I don't want you at my office *ever*." I rolled my eyes as I walked toward her.

"Lana, you can't tell me what to do. Do you think you're better than me because you got a little office or some shit? You ain't no better than me. Deep down, you are *just* like me. You and Rebecca are just like me. You know why, because we're triplets." Dareen slammed the mini fridge shut, then stood up, looking directly at me.

"I'm *nothing* like you, Dareen, and neither was Rebecca. If anything, *you* were the rotten one that came out of our mother. I would *never* want to be like you." I went closer into her personal space.

"Bitch, you coming up on me like you wanna do something. What you gonna do, huh?" Dareen shoved me in the chest, making me stumble back.

"Dareen, stop it. *Don't* touch me again," I yelled as she continued putting her hands on me.

"Stop what, Lana? Stop doing this?" She shoved me harder that time so that I fell on the floor.

"You are *not* my sister. And when all of this is done, I want you out of my life for good," I shouted, while getting off the floor.

"Listen, if you stick to the fucking plan, this will be over with sooner than you think. You think I want to be close to someone who doesn't love me? Never have. What kind of sister are you?" Dareen threw my green glass vase at me, striking me in the arm.

"Dareen, stop this! I never said I didn't love you. Me and Becca may have loved you the most! But you always pushed us away, acting like this. Maybe I should refer you to someone like me," I suggested, backing away from her and the shattered glass all over the floor.

"I need to see a shrink 'cause I'm crazy? *That's* what you trying to say? You think I'm crazy? You're so worried about me, but forgetting about the people who killed our sister." Dareen cornered me by the edge of my desk.

"I don't believe Tommy killed anyone. Especially not Becca. I honestly don't know if you have told me everything. But you are right about focusing more on the truth and getting Rebecca justice," I said back to her.

Dareen leaned down, slicing my leg with a piece of glass. "I want everything Tommy has ever said to you. I want whatever recordings and notes you have. *I* will deal with Tommy."

"I can't do that. Client-patient confidentiality. I can tell you what may be public record." My leg was bleeding, and I didn't want it getting on my white carpet.

Dareen was irritated with me and my response. Stepping over me, she pulled out all of my drawers, tossing the papers everywhere. When she located Tommy's file in the third drawer, she stopped suddenly, and I knew she had found it. I had no clue that she would come to my office and go through my things.

"You had to make it so difficult." Dareen slapped me with the folder, then walked away.

"I hate you," I mumbled as I fought back the angry tears that were threatening to come out.

"I love you too, sister. I'll see you when you get home. Enjoy the rest of your day." She shut my office door.

I looked around before getting up and seeing that Dareen was gone. I probably should've hit her back, but I didn't want to get physical with her. I was mad at myself for letting her get access to Tommy's info. I needed to get it back before she did something crazy.

My sister's mind was unstable, and there's no telling what she would attempt to do. As I cleaned up the mess she made, my hands landed on the sticky note with

Tommy's number and address. I placed it on my desk and finished getting my office in order.

After everything was back in place, I grabbed the sticky note with my briefcase and rushed out the door. I was taking a huge chance by going to Tommy's home, but I needed to see him. I wanted to make sure he was okay and also see what answers he could provide me about both of my sisters. If Dareen was right about anything, it was that Tommy was needed. He was the key.

CHAPTER EIGHT

Tommy

"Oh, fuck yeah. Shit, Tommy . . . Damn, daddy, that's it! Mmmm, yeah, baby, right there," Rayna moaned out as I pounded her pretty phat ass from behind.

"You gonna ride this dick, huh?" I grabbed her long, blond tracks with one hand, roughly tossing my dick into her.

"Yes, yes. Let me ride it." Rayna was a true champ. She took this dick every way I gave it to her.

Her beautiful frame looked even more amazing outside that little outfit she had to wear at the bar where I met her. Yeah, I was smashing the waitress from a few nights ago. For once, my boys were right. Since we started fucking around, I hadn't thought about Dareen so much. My nuts were always empty because shorty liked to get dicked down on a regular, several times a day.

I could feel her body getting ready to come for me as she screamed out, "Make me come, baby. Make me fucking come. Oooh yeah, fuck, Tommy. Tommy . . ."

"Shut the fuck up and take this dick." I gripped her waist and beat her walls down.

I tossed my dick in her like I was a porn star. Her body shivered as I kept fucking her hard and fast. The more she begged me to stop, the harder I went. My nut was rising to my head, and I was about ready to explode. I pushed her off of me, then straddled her face and told her to take my nut.

"Tell daddy you want his nut," I instructed while jacking my dick in her face.

"Daddy, I want that cum." Rayna sounded so sexy the way she moaned out how she wanted my nut.

"Here it comes. Don't fucking move." I jerked as I unleashed my load over her face and hair.

I watched her reach for the towel that hung over my nightstand to wipe off her face. While we were trying to recover, I thought I heard someone knock on my door. I checked my phone to see if Eric or Joe had texted me, and when I saw no notifications but Facebook, I let whoever it was go away.

It was a Saturday, so maybe it was the Jehovah's Witnesses. They have no time limit and will always pop up. When the knocks came louder and harder, I told Rayna to pass me the towel. Wrapping the towel around my waist, Rayna bit her lip, then told me to hurry back for round two.

Slowly opening the door, I saw my therapist standing there. I was in complete shock when I saw her. "What are you doing here?"

"I wanted to check on you. You missed your sessions. I wanted to make sure everything was okay," Dr. Morane stated, peeping around me, trying to look into my home.

Stepping outside, I closed the door behind me so Rayna wouldn't hear our conversation.

"Everything is good, really. Dr. Morane, please don't come to my house unannounced. When I'm ready to set my appointment, I'll call your office."

"Tommy, you don't think we need to talk? We haven't spoken since, you know." She reached her arm out, letting her left hand brush seductively down my arm.

"Listen, I'm busy right now. We can talk some other time." I backed away from her, leaning toward my door. The brisk wind hit my body, making my dick shrivel up.

"Tommy, please. I want to talk . . ." Dr. Morane was still trying to have a conversation with me.

"As I said, I'm busy. I'll call you." I went back inside, slamming my door in her face.

I wasn't sure what she wanted to talk about, but it wasn't my top priority. I went back into my bedroom, where Rayna was puffing on one of my cigars, dressed in my throwback high school football jersey. I watched her put out the cigar, then crawl to the edge of the bed. I came closer to her, dropping my towel to the floor, waiting for her to make the next move.

She grabbed my legs so my dick could slap her face. Rayna tickled my balls with the tip of her tongue while I stroked my dick, making it stand tall.

"Put this dick in your mouth," I ordered as I tapped the head of it on her lips.

Rayna opened her mouth wide, allowing my dick inside her mouth. As she inhaled it, it stretched inside her mouth while she held her breath and gobbled it up so it could hit her tonsils. I stroked my dick in and out of her mouth while holding her head for balance.

"That's it, baby, suck this dick. Mmmm, fuck, yeah. Suck this shit," I moaned while feeling her wet, slippery mouth around my shaft.

Rayna was giving me the best head I ever received. I was in complete ecstasy when a shadow appeared outside my bedroom window. I jumped back, wondering if it was her, Dareen, and if her spirit was watching me. Maybe it was coming for me. I made Rayna stop sucking me off and crept over to the window, dick in hand. I peeked out of the right corner of the window, but nothing was there.

"Bae, what you doing?" Rayna followed me to the window, then got on her knees to finish the job.

Letting out a soft groan, I said, "There was something at the window. I thought I saw something."

Lifting her head, Rayna smiled. "Whatever it was must be gone. Now, focus."

Picking Rayna up from the floor, I yanked my shirt off her. I was ready to fuck again. I watched her play with her pussy, getting it wet and ready for me. Her moans were pleasing to my ears, and I was going to make her scream. I propped her body on the windowsill, where she wrapped her legs around my waist. Once I had her positioned properly, I slammed my dick inside of her.

She clawed my back while I stroked her pussy. If anyone was watching, they were getting quite a show. I pulled out before she came again and turned her body to face the outside of the window. Her perfect C-cup chest pressed against the clear windows as I spread her ass cheeks and slid in from behind. Then I grabbed her neck, choking her just a tad, causing Rayna to arch her back slightly, allowing me to slow stroke her. While I gave her every inch of my rod, I bent down and licked her from the crack of her ass to her neck.

We could see people walking or driving by, noticing our sexcapade. The thrill of them watching us only made me go harder. Grabbing her hair like a leash, I pounded her pussy until I was ready to come. The louder she screamed my name, the less control I had. Moments later, I was exploding my legacy all over her ass cheeks.

After our last round, I was exhausted. Rayna sparked her blunt and cuddled up underneath my arms. We watched *Iron Man 3* until I passed out. I awoke in a dark place. Rayna was nowhere in sight. I wasn't sure where I was or what was happening to me.

"Rayna! Rayna, where are you?" I screamed, looking around me.

"She's not here, Tommy," a voice whispered from the dark.

"Who's there? Where am I? What's going on?" I got up from my bed.

"All will be revealed, but first, let's take a trip." The voice echoed in the dark room, sounding like a woman's.

As I stood in one spot, the lights came on, and I was in the warehouse again. I could see Dareen in the chair, begging for her life.

"Dareen, this isn't funny! Please, leave me alone!" I shouted, but no one said anything back to me.

I felt a force hit my back, making me fall on the concrete floor. Dareen was in the chair, and she looked at me with tears running down her face as another version of Dareen stood in the corner.

"No, please, don't kill her! Can't we do this another way, guys? Listen to me," I begged, pushing myself off the ground. I ran over to stop Reneece from slicing her throat, but she disappeared.

"Tommy, you killed the wrong person," Dareen said to me as her tears turned from water to blood.

"Dareen, baby, I'm sorry. I should've tried harder to save you." I got on my knees, holding her legs as I belted out my regrets.

"I am not *Dareen. My name is Rebecca. Rebecca is my name," she shouted at me while breaking free from the bondage that had her bound to the chair.*

The other image of Dareen appeared, but not just one extra image—two. I was baffled by what I was seeing.

"No, stop lying to me. Your name is Dareen. I won't fall for your tricks. I loved you, but you didn't love me." I backed away from the three Dareens, only for them to appear right behind me.

"We are not one. We are three. Out of three, you killed the one who resembled Dareen. Vindicate me. Then *you will be free. Tommy, you shall be happy again, once the true Dareen is found and justice for me, her sister Rebecca, is served." The three of them merged into one body, leaning over to hug me before disappearing.*

I woke up seeing Rayna's body facing the right side of the bed. Her snoring was the indication that I was, in reality, there. My mind felt scrambled as I tried to decipher my dream. Was there truth in what I just saw, or was it just my mind playing tricks on me? Getting up from the bed, I grabbed a pair of my black-and-white Polo Ralph Lauren boxers from my dresser drawer, sliding them up so I wouldn't be bare walking around the house.

While Rayna slept peacefully, I went into my living room to call a friend of mine in public records. I remembered that Dareen was in Durham for a while, so maybe I could find out a little more about her family. If there was any truth to my dream, we had killed the wrong person, and if I could reach Dareen in time, we could run away and have our happily ever after.

CHAPTER NINE

Lana

It had been a week since I showed up unannounced and clearly unwelcome at Tommy's home. I was still in complete shock, but yet turned on by what I witnessed there that day. After Tommy slammed the door in my face, which was completely disrespectful, I chose to see what was going on in his home.

I snuck to the back of the house, peeking inside the windows, and I watched him receive fellatio from some chocolate bitch who wasn't me. When he looked up, I thought he saw me, so I ducked down into the bushes that surrounded the outer black windowsill. I wanted to knock on his door again and confront him, but then I *would* look crazy. Considering he was just my patient and I had a weak moment, I was out of line again watching him, but I couldn't help myself.

I stuck my head up to see inside, but the woman's ass was now plastered on the windows. I could barely hear any of the sounds, but the way her back hit the windows, I could tell she was getting fucked good. Then what made it worse was that I watched him fuck her from behind. Part of me believes she saw me rubbing my pussy at them, the way she smiled. It was like she smiled at me before her mouth opened like she was gasping for air. I could only imagine what she was feeling, how good his dick felt.

I masturbated on his lawn to the two of them fucking until I climaxed. Forgetting that it was broad daylight by the time I came, I suddenly saw a man watching me from his cherry-red Dodge Challenger. Ashamed of myself, I scurried out of the bushes and ran back to my car. The man tried to stop me, but I had already overstayed my welcome.

I didn't know what was coming over me. Tommy was overpowering my thoughts, my actions, and my emotions. I have never been this way about anyone else before, especially a man who wasn't mine. One thing I couldn't figure out was who the woman was at Tommy's house. He never mentioned anything about a lover or girlfriend in our sessions. I need to know where she came from and get her out of my way. If Tommy was looking for a true companion, he has me. I figured once I found out the truth about what happened to Rebecca, Tommy and I could be together.

I took the next few days playing undercover and paying a private eye to get more information on this trick. I eventually found out she worked at Buffalo Wild Wings and at this strip club called Diamond Girls. Then I located her full name, address, birth date, parents' information, and so forth. I created a fake profile on Facebook and added her as a friend to see what kind of shit she was on. The girl was only 24, and from the looks of it, she wasn't that educated. I thought to myself, *Why would Tommy want anyone like her when he could have me?*

Obviously, Tommy was blind. So, I needed to make him see, but in a subtle way. I needed a game plan because if she were going to be difficult about the situation, she would have to leave the *hard* way. I knew the only person who would have my back and could pull off something crazy was the one person I barely wanted to deal with: Dareen.

It was a Friday evening when I came home from a long day at work. Dareen was sitting right where I'd left her, on the couch. She looked as if she hadn't taken the time out to even groom or bathe herself today. I had to figure out a way to get Dareen to come with me to the club tonight. I figured it was the perfect night to end that girl's fling with my man.

I went over and sat on the couch beside her while she watched *Poetic Justice*.

"Had a good day at work, sister?" Dareen asked, keeping her eyes on the television.

"It was long, sister. Did you do anything today? Any leads?" I attempted to make small talk with her.

"Not right now. Maybe soon. Just keep working on Tommy. I'm going to start looking at things with that Eric dude." Dareen grabbed her Dasani water bottle from the floor and opened it to take a sip.

"Well, I was thinking we could go out tonight. I know I haven't been the best host or sister since you came around, and I want us to get to know each other again and have some fun." I hope she couldn't tell I was putting on a front.

"Really? Or you tryin'a get me back from the other day at your office?" Dareen turned, looking at me suspiciously.

Turning my body to face her completely, I said, "No, this is real shit. We can't get justice for our fellow sister if we are at odds with each other. And to be honest, I can understand where you were coming from, and I definitely was wrong. Let's just start over."

"Okay, cool. Where did you want to go?" I had won Dareen over, and I was ecstatic.

"I was thinking maybe the party I heard about in Chapel Hill, and then we can end our night at a strip club. Maybe grab us a nigga or two," I laughed out loud.

"Well, we kinda the same size. Do you have something I can wear tonight? 'Cause I sure 'nuff don't have any club clothes. If that's okay?" my sister asked, looking in my eyes so sincerely.

I nodded and told her to follow me to the bedroom so she could go through my closet and try on a few pieces that caught her eye. I can't lie. As we both tried on outfits, it reminded me of when we were kids and used to play fashion show with our aunt's clothes. We always made one another look as fly as possible.

After we finally picked out our 'fits for the night, Dareen volunteered to cook dinner for us. I wasn't sure if she was going to try to poison me or what. Shit, I knew my sister had some crazy tendencies, and I knew being on her good side for now was going to be worth it in the end.

Sis did her thing in the kitchen. She made stovetop mac, baked chicken, and rice. I was glad it wasn't spaghetti because even though I'm all woman, I've heard 'bout that period blood in the food trick, and I don't need her trying that disgusting thing on me.

After we ate and had a few glasses of red wine, Dareen and I started to get ready for our night on the town. The house was full of music as we drank and helped each other with our makeup and hair. Two hours later, we were ready. Dareen asked if we could take a couple of pictures before we left.

Grabbing my blue iPhone 5c, I turned the camera to front mode and took several videos and pictures of us. The only request she had was that I not post them on social media. She wanted to keep them for herself. When she asked that, I was a little apprehensive about what it meant. However, instead of trying to get into her business, I agreed so our night wouldn't turn into a disaster.

We arrived at Club Paradise in Chapel Hill around eleven thirty that night. The line wrapped around the corner, but luckily, I knew not only the security but also the promoters.

"Sis, we'll be in line all night before we get inside," Dareen's said while her eyes were glued to the window watching the line as I drove to the back of the building for parking.

"Hell no, girl. Our way in is just a phone call away. I rarely stand in anyone's line when I go out," I chuckled while pulling into the first open parking spot I saw.

"You got it like that?" My sister seemed shocked that I had any connections, let alone for parties.

"Damn, why so shocked?" I laughed. "Shit, sis, I mean, if niggas always tryin'a get the pussy, they gotta be able to do something for me. This nigga Don always wants to fuck, but I ain't into him like that. But I give him a good show. I'll introduce y'all when we go inside. You may like him."

"Okay, then, well, let me sit these itty-bitty tits up a little higher. See what I can catch tonight 'cause we some badass bitches, okay, sis?" Dareen blew me a kiss before pushing her breasts up higher until they almost popped out.

Every girl in the line turned their nose up at us when we walked right past them and into the club. Don and his business partner, Odyssey, were standing at the front when we came in. He was happy to see me there, but when I introduced him to my sister, he was all over her.

The club was half-packed, but the DJ was bumping some good music. Don ordered us a bottle of our choice while he attended to his host duties. Dareen was taking shot after shot while dancing to every song that came on.

"Sis, come on, dance with me," she begged while holding her hands out to me.

Dream's "Rockin' That Shit" played in the background. I couldn't lie. That was one of my favorite songs by him. I swallowed my shot before grabbing her hand. We danced together to the song until Don came back over, directing his focus back on Dareen. I was happy he wasn't focusing on me. He never turned me on, but watching the two of them together made me think twice. They were dancing really sexually, to the point where you would think that they were fucking on the dance floor.

"Y'all should just get a room," I teased while locking eyes with a tall, chocolate fellow who was passing our way.

"You gonna let me take your sister home?" Don yelled over the music.

Dareen came over and sat on my lap before replying, "You can see me when we leave the strip club later."

Don came over asking Dareen for her phone so he could put his number in it. Once the two of them exchanged numbers, we headed out the door before they turned on the lights. Part one of our night was a success, and Dareen had the widest smile on her face while Don walked us to the car.

Our next stop was the strip club, and it was time to handle business accordingly. All the while I was driving, I was trying to come up with a plan in my head. We stopped at Cookout off Miami Drive to grab a quick bite to eat before going to Diamond Girls.

Diamond's parking lot was super tight, barely any parking available, so we parked on the side of the street and decided to walk up. Once inside, the crowd was lit, and money was flying in every direction. I would be a liar to say I didn't pick up a twenty or two that landed in my path. Shit, it was free money.

Dareen spotted us a table near the back of the club that was just cleaned off by one of the waitresses. As time went on . . . and on, there was still no sign of the girl Tommy was fucking. I was getting irritated, hoping to see her, so I decided to take a bathroom break to gather my thoughts.

I walked into the women's bathroom, and it was so disgusting. Wet toilet paper was scattered across the floor, and what I assumed was alcohol covered the tiles. I tiptoed around the dirty spots to the stalls. One stall had a bloody tampon in it, one had pee over the toilet seat, and the third one I found was the cleanest, so I squatted over the toilet seat and let my piss drain out.

While I was peeing, I heard a group of girls come in, conversing about their friend's new piece of dick.

"Girl, that nigga's dick is just so long and thick. It barely fits up in this tight-ass pussy, but I take all of it like a champ," one girl told her friends.

"Shit, bitch, I love me a big-dick nigga. He got any big-dick friends?" another voice asked.

"Rayna, the real question is, are we gonna get to meet him? Maybe we can share like we did ole boy, with the dreads," her other friend chimed in.

When I heard the name Rayna, I knew it was her, but I had to make sure before I went off. I stayed in the stall for a few more moments, eavesdropping. The girl, Rayna, finally dropped her boo thang's name: Tommy. When she described how he looked to her friends, that was my indication that I finally found the ho responsible for taking my Tommy away from me.

I wanted to catch a glimpse of her before walking back to the floor. After wiping my ass good, I used my foot to flush the toilet, straightened my clothes, and went out to the main area of the bathroom with the marble sink counters. As I washed my hands, the girls were still talking about Tommy. The more the Rayna chick talked about their sexcapade, the angrier I got.

"Excuse me, I couldn't help but overhear your conversation. It sounds like you're talking about my man," I said loudly as I washed my hands.

"Excuse me? Who are you talking to?" Rayna stepped out of the circle of her friends while looking at me through the mirror.

Turning to face her, I said, "Tommy Malachi Fosierie is my man. Stay away from him. I'm asking nicely."

"If he was your man, why is it that I stay at his house six days a week? He's in my sweet little pussy every chance he gets. If anything, he's *my* man. You must suck him off or something on his breaks when I can't get to his job." Rayna insulted me by considering me the side piece. She must have lost her mind.

"Bitch, I will fuck you up." I took off my gold hoop earrings and placed them on the counter before getting in her face.

"Ho, you funny. I'll tell my man to get his hoes in check. And before you even touch me, think about my backup over there." Rayna's stripper friends came over to our space, crowding around her.

As we stood toe-to-toe, I heard my name being called. Dareen came in and saw the girls surrounding me.

"Sis, the fuck is happening here?" she asked, walking in slowly, sizing up each girl.

"They trying to jump me because this bitch right here still mad that her ex is with me and not her," I lied to cover my tracks, but it wouldn't matter because Rayna was about to be taught a lesson. "Dareen, even when I told her to leave me and him alone back then, she wouldn't. I don't even have that nigga no more, and she still mad."

"Bitch, you a fucking liar. Girls, let's teach these two bimbos a lesson," Rayna instructed.

Before anyone could swing, Dareen had taken off. Her friend, in nothing but a black G-string, was knocked out cold on the bathroom floor after Dareen slammed her head against the wall. Rayna and I went at it. Blow for blow, we took jabs at each other.

As the brawl broke loose in the bathroom, Security was called in by another partygoer who was just trying to pee. Once we were separated, Security kicked us out, and I was pissed off that I couldn't really spark fear in that ho like I wanted.

"Those hoes looked scared as fuck. They thought you were alone," Dareen said as she held my arm as we walked down the rocky hill back to the car.

"Yeah, I guess she was surprised. Thanks for having my back, sis." I felt warm inside, knowing how Dareen came to my defense without any instigation.

"Regardless of what has or hasn't happened, you're still my sister. I'll always have your back." Dareen pulled me in for a hug once we got to the car.

Now, even though I was still suspicious of the story she told me about Rebecca, she showed me a different side of herself tonight. I felt as if I should give my sisterhood another chance. I needed to trust her and, most importantly, love her. We headed back home with a few bumps and bruises, but our relationship was starting to mend.

CHAPTER TEN

Eric

I came to work feeling great. It had been a few weeks since I had hung out with the fellas. Reneece was finally home where she deserved to be, and our daughter was growing healthy. I couldn't be happier. This was my first time back in the office since my wife came home, and it had me walking in with a little pep in my step, knowing things seemed to be getting better.

Before I could head to my office door, my assistant stopped to warn me that Tommy had come in today as well. I hadn't been sure if Tommy had been back the whole time I was gone or if it was a coincidence that he came back today. Even though we seemed to be fine after our boys' night, I couldn't care less about anything Tommy wanted if it wasn't anything positive or business related. Heading to my office, I stopped by his office and saw that he looked like himself. He was dressed well in a tailored suit, had a fresh haircut, and was focused on his laptop. My mans was working, and that's what I liked to see.

I waved at my friend and business partner, then headed across the hall to my office. It seems as if Tommy had been there while I was gone and landed us a contract to reconstruct an old warehouse into what the owners were calling a "Nightclub with a more sexual twist." I read between the lines and realized they wanted to have a sex club. To be honest, I thought it was a dope concept, and the money they were talking about had so many figures, I couldn't care less about anything else.

Doing what I do best, I got to work, reaching out to our new clients to arrange a meeting so we could see the possible space with my engineers and estimate how much it would cost for repairs and such. The day was going by smoothly. I did call home frequently to check on Reneece, like when we placed our daughter in day care.

It was around one thirty that afternoon, and I was about to break for lunch when Tommy came tapping on my glass office door.

"Hey, man, come on in! I was going to come by and thank you for locking in our new clients. This project and the money for it, man, you did that." I closed my laptop so we could talk.

"E, man, it was the least I could do. I haven't done my part, and I was still getting paid, you know? So, I had to come back strong," Tommy stated as he came into the office, leaving a slight crack in my door when he closed it.

"Listen, I want to say something. One, Reneece is awake and finally back at home. She even asked about how you were doing. Two, man, look, I know I haven't been easy to talk to when it comes to your feelings for that girl. I understand that you loved or maybe still love her a little, but I do wish that you get the help you need." Leaning back in my chair and looking at my friend, I noticed he seemed uncomfortable when I brought up Dareen.

Clearing his throat, he said, "That's awesome. Tell sis I'm getting better day by day. If you wanna talk about Dareen, I think there's something you should know."

"What's on your mind, bro? I promise I'll be open-minded and listen like a friend should," I assured him, so that I could figure out what was going on inside my friend's mind.

"A few nights ago, I had a dream. A crazy dream." Tommy took his hand and ran it across his head.

"Okay, what happened in it?" I asked, feeling intrigued about what this dream could have been about.

"So, basically, after me and Rayna, that waitress from the bar we went out to that night, remember her?" Tommy asked with a slick smile.

"Oh, you fucking shawty? Okay! That pussy got you feeling like a new man, huh?" I leaned over my desk to give him some dap.

"Yeah, man, she's cool, and she's a major freak, ya hear me?" Tommy shook his head and chuckled. "After a wild round of sex, we passed out, and I had this dream that maybe there's more than one Dareen."

"Tommy, the hell you talking about?" I questioned, wondering where he was going with this.

"Just listen. In the dream, the girl we killed came to me. She was in the chair, and instead of Reneece slicing her throat, Dareen did. Then all of a sudden, man, she appeared to me, *three* of them. After that, they all turned into one. So, what if the girl we killed wasn't Dareen but her sister or something?" Tommy's eyes widened before he rose from the chair.

"Tommy, if there were more than one of her, don't you think we would've known it by now?" I came from behind my desk, leaning against the wall.

"Eric, we have to look into this. Just for all of our sakes. If she still is alive and well, then we all have more to worry about, especially if we killed her sister." Tommy's voice got louder and filled with fear.

"All right, look, I'll make some calls. See what I can find out about her background or family. But what if you're wrong?" I said to him while moving in closer.

"Then we just move on, and I continue with therapy. But what if I'm right? What if my dream was a sign?" Tommy questioned as he stood up from his chair.

"If you're right, we've got to find a way to end all of this before more innocent people die. But I really hope you just had a bad dream." I walked back over to my desk and looked outside the window at the commotion down on the streets.

"Aye, bro, I got a meeting with my therapist too in like thirty. I'm gonna head out. If I don't swing back, I'll finish up my paperwork from home, and I'll see you in the office on Monday. But I'll call you and try to come to the house later to see y'all." Then Tommy scurried out of my office to his appointment.

After he left, my mind wandered. Deep down, part of me felt that maybe we'd caught the wrong chick, and, out of anger, we'd just offed her without hearing her out. She pleaded for us to listen, but we didn't. For the sake of our souls—and our lives—I'm praying Tommy only had a crazy-ass dream.

Tommy

I was happy to leave the office on a good note with Eric. I wanted to catch up with my little boo, Rayna, before seeing Dr. Morane. Shit, she was always down for a quickie or two in the middle of the day. That's one thing that kept me going back.

I called her phone several times, but she wasn't answering. I was five minutes from her job, so I did a pop-up to see if she could take a break. I knew when she was busy on the floor, she couldn't answer the phone. I pulled into the Buffalo Wild Wings parking lot and saw that a few cars were there. I parked beside this dark blue Lexus toward the front of the building. When I got inside, I saw her petite, thick ass standing by the bar.

Sneaking up behind her, I put my arms around her waist. "When is your break, beautiful?"

"Excuse me?" Rayna turned around, shocked to see it was me.

"When is your break? Let me get you right real quick; then you can stay with me tonight. Or stay with me forever." I attempted to place a kiss on her lips, but she backed away.

"I'm at work. That sounds nice and all, but your little girlfriend was at my job and jumped me. So, we can talk when I get off. I'm not in the mood right now. So, that's why I haven't been around, or haven't you noticed?" Rayna rolled her eyes as she leaned back against the bar.

"How can I have a girlfriend if I'm with you all the time? Come on, maybe she was a jealous ex. Wait, how did she even know you or you even know she was talking 'bout me?" I was puzzled and stood back, trying to put everything together.

"She gave me your whole name. Look, give me five minutes, and then we can talk outside. I'm parked in the back." She sighed deeply as she went to attend to a table of guests before leaving me at the bar.

I walked out to my car and drove to the back of the building, parking behind her silver Ford Focus. Her little attitude made my cock hard as a rock. I couldn't wait to get her into the backseat of my Mercedes-Benz Jeep. I was going to send her back to work walking funny. I didn't want to talk. All I wanted to do was bang her body out.

Five minutes went by, then there she came, swishing those little hips while she puffed on a cigarette. All I could think of was ripping those little bitty shorts off and sliding my tongue on her pussy lips. I honked my horn so she would come straight to me. Before she got inside the car, I unbuckled my pants, so I didn't have to waste any time. Rayna climbed in, still puffing on her cigarette that was halfway gone.

"Give me a kiss," I instructed, leaning over the armrest with my lips puckered up.

"I don't want to kiss you. I don't want anything from you, honestly." Rayna kept her body turned toward the passenger window.

Her mind was telling her to play like she didn't want me, but the way she clinched her legs together, I knew that pussy was calling me. I leaned over a little more so I could kiss her neck. As I sucked on her nips, Rayna moaned out no. Her moans only excited me more. Her hands reached for my pants, groping my dick.

"Tell me you want me, Tommy. Tell me you want this pussy," Rayna moaned out as my fingers went into her wetness.

"I want my pussy. This still my pussy, isn't it? Tell me it's still my pussy," I whispered in her ear as I dug my fingers deeper inside of her.

"Show me this your pussy, daddy. Show me." Rayna pushed my hands away. "Let's go home, so I can fuck you the way I want."

She didn't have to say that again. If your girl or the person you're intimate with has to tell you twice to come get it, then you ain't horny enough, or you really don't want them. Rayna said she would follow me, but first she would let them know she was leaving early. Twenty minutes later, we were speeding out of the parking lot, heading straight to my house.

My appointment with Dr. Morane would have to wait. I asked to reschedule for later this evening when I called her office. When we got to my home, we parked the cars all crazy, trying to get into the house. By the time we got inside, we were stripping each other at the door. As soon as I got her pants and tights off, I had Rayna's pussy all in my face, covering it with her juices. I lifted her body onto my shoulders with her back against the door. Swirling my tongue around her swollen clit, Rayna moaned out my name in between breaths.

I lowered her back on the floor, ready to feel my dick hit the back of her throat, but when she wanted to 69 in a handstand, I couldn't refuse. That was something I only saw on porn, but I was down to experience it myself finally. Rayna positioned her body just right so her mouth could stay on my dick. I watched her slob over my dick without gagging. As she tasted this caramel dick, I shoved my head in between her ass cheeks, eating her ass while my fingers played in her pussy.

Hearing the way she moaned with my dick inside her wet-ass mouth made me wanna bust immediately. But I had to stop her because I needed to punish her for holding that pussy from me for the past few days. We couldn't make it to the bedroom the first round. I pushed her body on the floor, then Rayna arched her back and waited for me to slide inside. I kneeled on the hardwood floors, getting another taste of her pussy before sliding my big-ass dick in her pussy. I was going to make her take all this dick. I pressed down on her lower back and slid my dick deep inside her.

I gave her a few pumps, then let my dick sit inside of her pussy so she could feel it pulsate against her walls. I moved my body in a circular motion so my dick could tap each wall she had. She reached back and gripped her ass cheeks as I drilled my dick balls deep in her pussy, hard and fast. I was showing that pussy no mercy. I was thinking with my dick and not my brain when I busted all inside her.

Rayna squirted my cum out of her pussy like a cream pie right before we collapsed on the floor, trying to catch our breath.

"I guess if you were waiting on me, there really is no girlfriend, right?" Rayna was panting like a dog when she lay her head on my chest.

"No girlfriend. Like, how did you get something like that? Unless it comes from me directly, it's just me and you, shorty. I even got a key made for you." I tapped her shoulders for her to sit up so I could get back up.

I reached into my brown glass bowl, grabbing a Pandora box out of it. I opened it, showing her the gold and silver heart charm alongside the house key that I made for her. Rayna jumped into my arms, full of glee.

"I really got a key to your house?" Her eyes glistened with joy.

"Yeah, if you want it, baby," I responded with a wink.

"Hell yeah, I do." Rayna pulled me close, landing a nice, sloppy kiss on my lips. "Let's go to the bedroom. Tell your doctor you're going to reschedule."

I didn't consider her my girlfriend, but it was nice to have a woman who was all about me again. I followed her into the bedroom for another round before my appointment, and the way she guided me there told me she was going to go all out to thank me.

CHAPTER ELEVEN

Dareen

Lana was keeping a huge secret from me, and I figured it out when I followed that girl to work. We fought at the club a few nights ago. When I saw Tommy come through there, I just thought it was a coincidence, but it was more than that. See, after our little scuffle, I decided to be a good triplet and handle that ho. So, I gathered my own little intel on this Rayna girl to handle this roach-looking bitch for my sister.

I was sitting in the blue Lexus when Tommy pulled up in his Benz truck. I was shocked to see him there, but it made my day even more interesting. I followed behind him in the restaurant to see if he was meeting Eric. I needed to see him. But it wasn't a guy he was meeting. It was that ho from the club. He left after she dismissed him, so I followed him, and when I got there, I saw them fucking in his house through his front window. He was banging the fuck out of her on the floor.

So, I figured Tommy must have been telling this ho some unnecessary shit. Now, it felt as if Lana had lied to me. She must have known all along about this girl, and that she knew about me or what happened to Rebecca. I didn't understand why she didn't just tell me the truth instead of lying and trying to handle the situation on her own.

After watching them fuck, I snuck back to my car. While I waited for the girl to leave, I took out my phone and searched through my email looking for a video I made secretly one of the nights me and Eric fucked in his house. Man, he was so busy worrying about sliding up in this puss he didn't realize I had broken into the house earlier to set up a camera.

I took out my dildo I had made in the shape of Eric's dick and watched the video. Stroking it in and out of my pussy slowly, I watched how Eric fucked my asshole while rubbing my pussy with his fingers. I moaned out his name while I pumped that chocolate, nine-inch thick dildo into my pussy. My pussy enjoyed every hard thrust I gave it. I fucked myself until I creamed, and my body shivered in pleasure.

After I busted that well deserving nut, I realized Tommy's car was gone. It was about nine that evening when Rayna came out of the house. I followed her slowly, hoping I could catch her off guard. We were on the highway, and it was so empty. There was not a cop in sight, so I sped up a bit. I hit ninety-five miles per hour and rammed the back of her car, tapping her bumper and making her speed up even more. Chasing her was such a thrill. I roared my engine, gearing up to a hundred miles per hour as I hit her car with all the force possible. Her car jerked, but she was still going. I pulled up beside her and slammed her vehicle on the passenger side. Rayna put on her signal to exit the highway, and I took that as my shot. I fell back a little to let her get ahead.

Rayna was exiting the ramp when I rammed into the car from behind. That last hit I gave her car did it. The car spun out of control, and the hood slammed into the guardrail. I backed up and left the aftermath before another car came. As I drove down to the next exit, I grabbed my burner phone and called 911.

"911, how can I help you?" the operator answered.

"Yes, I'm traveling down NC 147, and a car has spun out of control and hit the guard rail on the South Point exit." I tried to sound concerned.

"Ma'am, can you give me your name, and are you still at the scene?" the operator asked.

"No, I'm on my way to work, but I called as soon as I saw it," I told her while merging on the side of the road.

The operator asked me several more questions while tapping on her keyboard. I pretended my phone was losing service as I tossed it out the window. I did my part. Hopefully, that ho was dead or severely injured. She'll think twice about meddling in our business if she survives the crash.

Lana

Tommy arrived in my office around seven thirty, and I had been anticipating his arrival. I sat in my office with nothing on but my silver blouse, fishnet stockings, and my red stilettos. I was going to show him everything he's been missing. He came inside my office looking better than I had ever seen him before. With his fresh low cut, he wore a black fitted T-shirt over straight-leg jeans, paired with his all-black Tims, and his clothes reeked of his Gucci cologne.

"Hey, Dr. Morane, thanks for still letting me see you this evening. Sorry I had to reschedule at the last minute." Tommy went to the mini fridge and grabbed a bottle of water.

Sitting at my desk, I looked at him with a smile. "Well, you look good. Plus, you don't smell like liquor."

Tommy laughed loudly. "Well, you know I've been getting some good rest and other things the past couple of weeks. So that helped."

"Well, that's good to hear. So, tell me what's the reason for your visit?" I moved from behind my desk.

Tommy almost choked on his water when he noticed my attire. I wanted to hop on top of him right there, but I needed to toy with him a little more. I sat in front of him in my brown leather chair, crossing my legs with my black leather notebook in my hand.

"Dr. Morane, where are your clothes? I came to talk about my issues, not get no pussy. I just got some before I came here." Tommy threw that little bitch in my face.

I had to play as if I didn't know who she was. "We can talk about that. I'm glad you are getting fucked, sir. The real question is, does her pussy feel as good as mine?"

"I wanted to talk to you about this dream I had, and even though I'm messing with someone, I still miss and love my former girlfriend. Sometimes, I feel that she's still here." Tommy cleared his throat as he tried to look away from me.

"Well, let's talk, shall we? I'm open." Spreading my legs open, I dropped my notepad so I could use my hands to travel up my thighs to my sweet spot.

Tommy couldn't take his eyes off me. He began biting his bottom lip as I teased him with my playfulness. I had him. He wanted me, and I knew it. I stood up, unbuttoning my blouse slowly so he could get a real show. Just as my shirt dropped to the floor, Tommy received a phone call.

"Hello? Yes, I am Tommy Fosierie. Is she okay? I'm on my way. Thank you." Tommy ended the call and gathered his things.

"Wait. Where are you going?" I asked, rushing to his side, trying to block him from leaving.

"I have to go. My girlfriend was in a horrible accident. I have to go. I'll come back tomorrow." Tommy pushed me to the side, then walked to the door.

"Tommy, wait, please. She can wait. Just stay with me." I blocked my office door, attempting to entice him, but Tommy wasn't falling for it.

"We can talk tomorrow." He gently pushed me out of the way and left.

Sexually frustrated, I slammed the door shut behind him. I couldn't believe he rushed to that little heffa's side. What could she possibly do for him that I couldn't, or more? I lay on my chaise, put on my panties, and tried to wrap my mind around everything. While lying there, my office door opened, and a shadow appeared in all black.

"Yes, can I help you?" I asked, sitting up quickly.

"Damn, sis, you act like you couldn't tell it was me." Dareen closed the door before stepping into the office.

"Girl, I couldn't tell who you were. And you didn't say anything." I took the water bottle Tommy barely drank out of and took a sip of my own.

"I did it. I took care of our little problem from the other night." Dareen sat on my desk, examining my attire. "Where are your clothes?"

"I was changing, then you came in," I lied, trying not to let my secret feelings for Tommy slip out.

"Mmm-hmm, look like you dressed to get some dick if you ask me," Dareen joked.

"Yeah, I wish. But what were you saying you handled? What did you do?" I questioned while searching in my closet in my office for my gym bag.

"That ho, Rayna. I found out she's seeing Tommy. Did you know that? Anyway, I ran her off the road, and now she's either severely injured or dead. No more worries 'bout *that* ho." Dareen let out a sinister laugh as if she enjoyed possibly killing that girl.

"I knew he was seeing someone and that he was confiding in her, but I had no clue it would've been the same girl. The world is hella small." I slid my yoga pants over my fishnet tights, feeling overjoyed that the girl may be entirely out of the picture.

"Well, now, we know. And if she did survive, I'll make sure she's silenced and won't try nothing crazy. I got us, sis. Don't worry." Dareen hopped off the desk and walked over to me with a smile.

"I know. We got each other. Let's grab something to eat. I'm hungry." I grabbed my Gucci bag to head out the door.

Either my sister trusted me, or she was playing along till she could kill me off too. Either way, I could now have Tommy to myself, and I could find out more about why he was seeing Dareen in his dreams.

CHAPTER TWELVE

Tommy

I arrived at the hospital and found Rayna lying on a hospital bed, almost unrecognizable. With only a distant relationship with her father, she really didn't have many people who cared for her, so I'm glad I was able to be by her side. I sat in the hospital room with her for three hours, praying for her to be all right until she died, still holding her hand. The doctors said they did everything they could, but they couldn't save her. I cried out to God, wondering why he was punishing me, when Dareen's image reflected in the hallway. I ran out to the hallway, but she was gone before I got there.

I left the hospital around three in the morning after they took her body down to the morgue. I was dumbfounded about what could have happened. Who would do this to her? It felt as if every time I got a glimmer of happiness, it was snatched away. I walked into the hospital's parking deck, and there she was again. Dareen was following me as I walked to my car.

"Stop following me! I *know* you did this. You did this, didn't you?" I screamed at her, but she said nothing back.

I reached my Jeep and looked around, but she wasn't there anymore. Dareen wouldn't let me be happy, and I knew why. It's because of what we'd done. I couldn't take it anymore. She was going to ruin my life. I hadn't had a drink since Rayna and I started fucking around, but I deserved one tonight. I reached into my glove compartment, and there was a bottle of Jack Daniel's, half-empty. I took the bottle straight to the head as I cried out for the two women I lost.

"Tommy . . . Tommy . . . Why didn't you save me? Tommy . . . Tommy . . . You were supposed to love me," I heard the faint voice say to me.

"Please, go away. I can't do this. I tried, Dareen, I tried," I blubbered out before taking another shot to the head.

I couldn't sit in that parking lot any longer. As I turned on my headlights, she appeared right in front of my car. I honked my horn and roared my engine, but she wouldn't budge. Cocking her head to the side, she winked at me. I knew I was drunk or gone mad. I buckled my seat belt, placed the lid on my bottle, and went straight ahead. As I drove out of the parking garage, I couldn't see her anymore. She was gone. Finally, she was out of my way. But for how long, I wondered.

I was heading home when Eric texted me. Since my phone was hooked up to the Bluetooth, it read out my messages.

Eric: Aye, bro, I just saw your text; call me.

Eric: Tommy, listen, man, you need to call me or Joe. Call somebody, man. We all at my house. Pull up.

I pulled over at a Circle K gas station to text him back.

Me: I'm not doing so well. But if y'all still up, I'm headed that way now.

Eric: Yeah, we here, bro. Come on thru.

Me: Bet. I'll see y'all soon. Tell Joe to roll one up for me.

I went inside the gas station and grabbed a twelve-pack of Bud Ice. Even if no one drank them with me, I would do so by myself. I arrived at Eric's house twenty minutes later, and his driveway was full. I parked in front of the street, then made my way to Eric's doorstep.

I knocked twice before Jalisa opened the door with welcoming arms. All I could do was howl in her arms. I felt defeated and alone. Her warm embrace reminded me that I still had friends. No, it reminded me I still had *family* who loved and cared about me.

I made my way into the living room to find Eric and Joe sitting there smoking a blunt. When Eric saw me, he passed it back to Joe, stood up, and reached his arms out to me.

"Bro, thanks for deciding to let us be here for you," he said as he gave me a brotherly hug.

"Yeah, I figured why be alone when I can be with family." I shrugged and walked over to Joe.

"Blood clot. Rude boy, ya come through and see ya fam. You want to hit this? This some good ganja, ya hear? Sit down." Joe passed me the blunt as he went back to his seat.

"We aren't going to wake Reneece, are we? I don't want to disturb her or the little one." I took two long hits from the blunt before sitting on the royal-blue sofa beside Eric.

"You mean baby? We're expecting another baby. I forgot to mention it." Eric winced as he told me the joyous news.

"Congrats, man! You guys are awesome parents. I'm happy for you both." I congratulated him, but part of me felt envious. I would've had a 1-year-old by now. I didn't get the chance to try to have a baby with Rayna. What did I do in my life to deserve such bad Karma?

"We are all sorry about Rayna, even though it was fresh you cared for her. We are sorry. We all are," Jalisa said to me as she sat on Joe's lap.

"Thank you. It means a lot." I leaned back on the sofa feeling weary. I closed my eyes, and there, Dareen appeared again.

The three Dareens turned into one over and over. They kept saying we "killed the wrong one. Save us. Set us free." Not knowing where I was anymore, I jumped up from the sofa, looking around. Eric, Joe, and Jalisa were staring at me with their eyes wide open.

"What's everyone staring at? I just realized I need to go piss." I walked past everyone in a hurry to the bathroom.

I splashed water on my face from the sink, trying to get my life together. When I emerged from the bathroom, everyone was sitting around, whispering. When I came around the corner, Eric stopped everyone from talking.

"Tom, you all right, man?" he asked, looking at me full of worry.

"Yes, I must have dozed off and had a bad dream or some shit. What were y'all talkin' 'bout in here?" I came back in, wondering what everyone was snickering about.

No one wanted to speak. The more they looked around, avoiding me and my question, the angrier I got.

"So, y'all was sitting around, talkin' about me or some shit? Y'all wanted me to believe y'all was my family. Loved me even, but y'all talking shit about me. Fuck all of you. Fuck you, fuck you, and fuck you, bitch," I shouted, grabbing my keys from my pocket and walking toward the door.

"Aye, you disrespect mi wife, you disrespect me." Joe jumped over the ottoman, lunging at me.

"What the fuck, bitch nigga? You wanna fight me? You still mad your bitch chose me instead of you? If Jalisa wasn't like a sister, I would take her from you too. Pussy nigga," I screamed as he came my way.

"Y'all two *stop* it. Stop it before you wake everyone else up. This is nonsense. Tommy, you are overreacting for nothing. Just calm down." Jalisa found her way in between us, trying to settle the storm that was brewing.

"Nah, I ain't overreacting. I asked all you bitches a question, and instead of answering me, you pretended not to hear me and sent texts to one another talking shit. Why can't you say it to my face? Huh? Y'all scared to say it to my face?" My frustration and anger increased by the second. I was nothing but a charity case and a joke to them.

"Tommy, you jumped up, screaming Dareen's name. We were discussing how to tell you about some information I found out. But not knowing what your mind state was in, we were choosing who should tell you." Eric came over to where Jalisa, Joe, and I stood.

My breaths were heavy, my fists were clenched, and I wanted to fight. It felt like I was being fed bullshit. Jalisa grabbed my hands and slowly caressed them to calm me down. I moved back from everyone, bumping into the wall.

"Tommy, whatever is going on in your dreams was right. I had Detective Peterson do some research for us, and so far, all we know is that Dareen is one out of a set of triplets. One was named Rebecca, then there was Dareen, and the other was named Laylani. So, she may be alive. We may have fucked up," Eric informed me after taking a deep breath.

"She's still alive? After all we did, and she's still alive?" Reneece's voice echoed from the dark corner by the stairs.

"Reneece?" Eric turned the hallway light on. "Baby, you should be sleeping."

"Well, how could I, when World War III was about to break out in my house?" Reneece was sitting on the bottom step, looking over at us.

Just like her, I was in shock. I wanted it to be true. I wanted to see and save my love. And to know there was a chance I could do just that made the darkness of my night brighter. Everyone's attention was redirected to

Reneece, so I took that as my escape. Yanking my hands from Jalisa, I rushed out of the house.

"Tommy! Tommy, come back," Eric yelled as I saw Joe running out the door behind me.

I left my so-called family and headed to Dareen's old apartment, hoping there would be answers there to heal me and to find her if she was still alive.

CHAPTER THIRTEEN

Eric

We couldn't stop Tommy from leaving my house tonight. I just hoped he didn't do anything crazy. After Jalisa and Joe left, I escorted my wife back into our bedroom. Reneece was silent the entire way up the stairs. I could only imagine what she was thinking. The one person who has caused her so much pain over the last two years may still be alive. Reneece had to be going through so many emotions.

Once inside our bedroom, I lay her back on the bed, and an awkward silence filled the air. I was unsure whether to say something. Reneece grabbed the remote from the nightstand and turned up the television volume before switching to HBO on-demand and searching for a movie to watch. I took off all of my clothing except for my boxers before plopping on the bed beside her.

"Babe, what you wanna watch?" I asked, trying to break the ice.

"Whatever's on, I guess. I ain't hiding anything—unlike you." Reneece cut her eyes at me.

"Listen, I didn't hide nothing from you. I promise you." I scooted closer to her, but she moved away.

Putting her hand in my face, she said, "Stop fucking lying to me. Tell me, how long did you know? Tell me the truth, Eric."

"I met with Tommy earlier today, or should I say yesterday. He told me about this dream and was worried about what the dream meant. I told him I would do some research. I hoped that nothing came back, but it did," I said, lying back on one of the pillows.

"Eric, so, it's true, she's alive?" Reneece's lip quivered as if she were about to cry.

"No, I don't know if she's alive. But she does have sisters. They were triplets. Now, with that knowledge, I have to make sure that we didn't kill an innocent woman for her sister's heinous actions." I pulled my wife into my arms as she started to cry.

"For all our sakes, I hope we didn't mess up. Eric, if she's still out there, you think she'll come for us?" Reneece slowly ran her fingers across my chest.

"If, and only *if* that's the case, I will do everything to make sure you and our children are safe. Know that." I kissed the top of her head as she clicked play on *Poetic Justice.*

Reneece

The next morning, Eric came into the room rubbing, on my little baby bump. It was around ten thirty when I saw the breakfast tray with cheese grits, French toast, fresh fruit, a cup of coffee, plus my favorite cheese Danish that he had laid out for me.

"Good morning, husband." I stretched before sitting up in the bed.

"Good morning, my beautiful wife." Eric bent down, softly kissing my lips.

"I would give you some tongue, but you know morning breath and all." I chuckled, moving the covers back to get out of bed.

"Well, it's not like I haven't smelled it before. You have the best morning breath ever." Eric was truly buttering me up like he had something up his sleeve.

"So, a morning breath compliment plus breakfast in bed. What are you up to? Or should I say, what have you done?" I was feeling a little leery after our brief conversation last night.

Eric just walked away into the bathroom, not saying another word. Following behind him, I leaned against our white wooden bathroom door, watching him brush his teeth.

"What's on your mind, beautiful?" he questioned after spitting out his toothpaste.

"Are you going to work today or play detective?" Moving behind Eric, I grabbed hold of his waist.

"I'm doing both. I meant what I said. Reneece, we have another baby on the way, and Hailey is growing more and more each day. We can't-*I* can't allow her to harm you or our children. I need to put some things in order, just in case." Eric tapped my hands, then broke free of my grasp.

"Eric, what the hell do you mean 'get things in order'? What the fuck are you talkin' about?" I chased behind him down the stairs while he grabbed his items for work.

"Reneece, babe, everything will be all right. Eat your breakfast. I'll be home around one to check on you, okay? I love you. I gotta go. I'm late for a meeting." He rushed out the door to head to work, I supposed.

Eric was backing out of the driveway when I noticed a person draped in all black staring at our house from across the street, but I couldn't make out their face because they wore a hood, dark shades, and some sort of face mask. I wasn't sure whether it was someone in the neighborhood. Eric honked his horn at me three times, and I waved goodbye to him before quickly going into the house.

I locked all the doors and shut my blinds to feel safe. I secured my household by any means just in case that nut tried to show up. My anxiety was at an all-time high. I didn't feel safe knowing Dareen was possibly still lurking around. After making sure everything was secure, I made my way upstairs, brushed my teeth, and took a nice hot shower. I came out of the bathroom feeling a little more relaxed than before. I checked the food and found everything had gotten cold. I was making my way downstairs with the tray when I heard glass shatter.

I stopped on the stairs and froze. Quickly, I tiptoed back into my bedroom, set the tray down, raced out to get Hailey, then back to my room and looked around for something to block my door. We were being robbed in broad daylight. This was unbelievable. I moved my nightstand and reclining chair to block the door, thinking that they were sturdy enough to keep anyone out. Petrified at what might happen next, I grabbed my iPhone, put it on silent, and called Eric. I called him five times, but no answer. After my last call attempt, he texted me.

Eric: Babe, are you okay? I'm in a meeting with new clients and Tommy.

Me: Someone's in the house. I can hear them. They were breaking the glass.

Eric: What? What you mean? I'm calling the police. You get somewhere right now and hide. I'm ending this meeting now.

Me: Please hurry. Babe, I'm scared.

Just as I sent the last message, I could hear what sounded like a soft tone whistling as they were creeping up the stairs. They stopped suddenly, and I couldn't tell where they were anymore.

"Reneece? Reneece, you in here?" Jalisa was here, unaware of what was going on.

Thinking fast, I texted her, hoping I caught her before she got hurt.

Me: Jalisa, get out. Call 911. There's someone in here. I'm hiding upstairs.

Jalisa: Some sirens are approaching. Just hold tight. Are you okay? Are you somewhere safe?

Me: Yeah, I am. I'm gonna come out when I know it's safe.

Jalisa: Eric and Tommy just pulled up.

I waited for Eric to come upstairs. I was trembling with fear. I went downstairs a few moments later, only to see the madness. Looking at my living room from the bottom step, I saw pictures scattered across the floor. Our wedding photo had been torn up, and broken glass was scattered everywhere. On the wall across from the steps was a message written in what looked like blood. The message read out:

> *You will never be safe! Eric, I love you. We will be together soon.*

CHAPTER FOURTEEN

Dareen

I had to be more careful. I almost got caught in Eric's home before putting the fear of God in Reneece. I was so angry with myself. I parked my car in an empty garage with Brian McKnight's "Anytime" pouring from my stereo system. Reaching into my bra, I pulled out a picture I found in Eric's house of him and his frat brothers on the Greek plot. He looked ravishing in his Kappa Alpha Psi cardigan, black skinny jeans, and white shirt. Reclining the driver's seat back, I tossed my right leg on the dashboard before plunging my fingers into my pussy.

I reminisced about the last time we had sex. I used my right hand to grip my neck as if he were choking me. I stroked my fingers in and out as I screamed out his name. My pussy craved for our man's dick, but I knew the long wait would soon be over. Continuing my stroke, I let go of my neck as my climax approached. Putting four fingers inside my pussy like the thickness of his dick, I pounded my tight pussy until I creamed all over my hand.

"*You have to remind him of what he's missing,*" my reflection told me when I looked in my rearview mirror.

"There's no way to do that without getting caught," I said back to myself, not knowing what she was thinking.

"*This is not a debate. We follow him, learn his schedule like before, catch him somewhere in the dark, get some-*

thing to cloud his judgment, and we take what belongs to us. He misses and loves us. He's been settling for how long? Get it together, bitch." My reflection screamed, almost scaring me.

"Maybe we should just get them back for killing Rebecca, then disappear. I love him, but I'm tired of this. I don't know what I want to do anymore," I confessed, feeling conflicted in my thoughts.

"*You simple bitch. What have we taught you all these years? We need to get things in order. Obviously, you've forgotten who the fuck we are. This man has loved us all this time, and you think we should give up now? Either he stays with us, or we kill him too.*" My reflection scrunched its face up at me, looking so disappointed.

But they were right, I was losing my spunk and getting soft. There was no reason for me to give up on my relationship with the man I love. I finally got myself together and headed back to Lana's house. I left her there fast asleep, and I hoped she would still be there when I returned.

It was nice to have a bond with the most distant of us, finally. Lana used to be Laylani, and those are two different people. I guess when she started changing herself, her personality changed with it. See, when we were younger, she wasn't so uptight. She would sneak out of the house with us. We went to house parties with the high school kids. Shit, all three of us lost our virginity at the same time. Those were the good ol' days.

After our aunt died so suddenly, that's when she started acting differently. She refused to go to the same college as Rebecca and me. Then she went away and lied about the school she was going to, like she was trying to hide from us. Honestly, it broke my heart. I thought we all were so close. Rebecca became focused on her studies. She was such a band geek and barely made time for me.

So, the distance among the three of us grew more and more until it was like we were all strangers.

I reached Lana's house, but her car wasn't there. After parking my car, I noticed a small piece of paper held down by a rock on the doormat. When I went to read it, the wind blew the page up, exposing a house key. I took the note. It read:

Dareen, you have shown me what a true sister is. And I'm sorry I haven't done my best to trust you or appreciate you. I had a key made for you. I wanted to give it to you before I went to work, but you were already gone. God really works in mysterious ways. I'm glad to have you back in my life. I love you, triplet.

Laylani

Reading that short note filled me with emotions I hadn't felt in years. I even cried a little bit. Clutching the note close to my heart, I tried my new house key to see if it worked. It did. She really, legit, got me a key, and I couldn't have been happier. I entered the house feeling like a new page was turning in my life.

Walking to the bathroom, I slipped a piece of my clothing off along the way. Her full-length mirror, pinned to the wall, showed my reflection, telling me to stop. I never disobeyed myself because I didn't know what the repercussions would be if I did.

"You can't get soft on her yet. We don't really know if she has our back." Myself folded her arms, staring right back at me.

"No. I feel like you might be wrong this time. Laylani is my sister, and she loves me. We just read her note. We have to give her a chance. We can't just off her without at least making sure it's the right thing to do." I came to my sister's defense. Nothing in me made me feel like Lana was using me.

"You didn't care at first. She was a pawn; she's always been a pawn. Now, you love her again, and she loves you again? You are becoming weak around her. We need strength, encouragement, and loyalty. How loyal do you think she's going to be when she finds out the real *reason Becca is dead?"* myself screamed at me, pressing against the mirror as if she were coming out.

"She won't find out. I promise. I'm going to do everything I can to make sure everything is tied up, and we can go on with our lives. We won't die, and we won't go to prison," I assured myself. "I got this. And with you guiding me, how can I fail?"

My reflection moved back from the edge of the mirror and stood up straight. *"You're right, we aren't. But first we have company."*

"Huh?" I asked just as the doorbell rang.

I had no clue who it could've been. I know I wasn't expecting any company. I grabbed my Bob Marley T-shirt from the floor to cover my body as I went to the door. Looking through the peephole, I saw a medium-height, dark-skinned brother looking like Larenz Tate standing there. His perfect chocolate skin tone looked like a Hershey milk chocolate bar ready to be eaten up.

His knocks were so hard, and it only made me think about how hard he would fuck me if I gave him the chance. My reflection shook her head no from the corner of the glass picture frame that held a picture of Lana and her sorority sisters to the right of the door. That was her way of telling me not to open the door for our safety.

"Hello? Who's there?" I asked through the door, clenching the doorknob.

"My name is Jackson. I'm looking for Lana Morane. Is she available?" His voice was deep, like the man on Quiet Storm, but also familiar.

"Umm, no. I'm her cousin, Ashley. I'm in town to visit. I can try to call her real quick to see if I should let you in, 'cause she's at work," I responded, looking back through the peephole to get a better look at him.

"No, that won't be necessary, miss. I'll come by later or stop by her office. Thank you so much." I watched Mr. Jackson turn and walk back to his car.

I went over to the front room window, trying to catch a glance at him, but Jackson was already getting into his black Honda Accord. He sped off so fast I couldn't get his license plate information. It felt odd that someone Lana had never brought up before popped up at her house like that. It was time for some investigation.

I knew my sister was probably busy with clients, so I couldn't go to the office now. Going back to the bathroom, I ran the bathwater to a temperature just above the boiling point. My lavender bubble bath filled the bathroom with its aroma. I soaked in the tub, feeling so relaxed that I fell asleep. Suddenly, I couldn't breathe, and I was underwater. Someone was trying to kill me. I struggled and struggled to get up, but they overpowered me. Finally, I was released. Grasping hold of the tub's rim, I was able to lift myself up.

Breathing heavily and coughing up the water that filled my lungs, I reached for my towel to dry my face. My feet touched the tile on the bathroom floor, and I found it was covered in water. Quickly walking into the hallway, I rushed into the kitchen and grabbed a knife. Whoever was in this house was going to die before me. I checked every room, but no one was there. Even the front door was locked. Still not feeling safe, I dried myself and tossed on a pair of sweatpants and a T-shirt, then left the house, heading straight to Lana's job.

CHAPTER FIFTEEN

Lana

After finishing my last client, Tommy abruptly entered my office. He seemed distraught. Knowing why without letting on would be the hard part. Sitting at my desk, I waited for him to sit down before diving into a surprise session.

"Doc, I'm glad I caught you. We need to talk. The other day, when I was here and rushed out, my girlfriend was in a bad accident." He jumped up and paced in the middle of my office.

"Tommy, I'm so sorry to hear that. I didn't know you had a girlfriend or anything like that. Especially after the last one you refuse to talk about. How are you feeling?" I honestly was super giddy, not for his pain, but to know that my sister was able to execute a simple problem in Tommy's and my relationship.

"How am I feeling? How the fuck do you think I'm feeling? We didn't have enough time! Me and Monica didn't have enough time either. I couldn't save either of them. How is it that I can't be happy? It's like God is punishing me." Tommy broke down, kneeling on the floor, crying.

"Listen to me, Tommy." I came from around my desk to console him. "Listen, baby, I mean Tommy. God makes no mistakes, and we have to trust him and his process. All this is a test for you to grow stronger. And you *will* be stronger. I am your therapist, and if you let me, I can be your friend, or more. Just let me in."

Tommy placed his head in my bosom, letting out a scream while blubbering like a baby. I reached over him to my coffee table to grab my box of Kleenex, bringing it down to where we were sitting on the floor. Cradling him in my arms, I felt his pain and wanted to take it all away. Tommy needed me. He just needed to realize it. With all the pain he'd been holding on to, I could set him free, and I planned to do it.

"Tommy, please, I can help you. I can do and be everything to you. You are always safe with me." I pulled his face out of my chest so we could look at each other, face-to-face.

Tommy leaned in, kissing me slowly. God, just the kiss alone made my pussy throb uncontrollably. The kisses grew more and more intense, and I couldn't control them anymore. I pushed him back and quickly undressed. Tommy did the same, tossing his gray shirt on the floor. I was ready to hop on that long, massive cock he had in those briefs.

Tommy yanked me closer to him. "Dr. Morane, give me that pussy."

"No, I'm Lana. Say my name, Tommy," I whispered, lying on my back and spreading my legs wide, rubbing my pussy to get it ready for him.

"Tell me you want my dick, baby." Tommy kneeled in front of me, jacking his dick while I played with my pussy.

"I want you, daddy." I dug two of my fingers inside of my wetness as I moaned those words.

"That's right, baby, get that pussy ready for me. That's gonna be *my* pussy now." Tommy leaned over to suck my pearl while my fingers stroked him.

His mouth felt *so* good on my pussy. I couldn't wait to have him inside of me. Forcing his head back, I motioned for Tommy to get inside of me. He pulled my legs back to my ears, and his dick filled my insides. He pumped me in and out slowly. With every thrust, I felt him go deeper and deeper inside me. I dug my nails in his back, clawing at his skin. He moaned while hitting my G-spot. Our eyes locked, and then he pulled my face into his, biting on my bottom lip in between kisses.

Rolling over, making me get on top and in control, I gripped the base of his dick while I lowered myself onto him. I was in complete awe of how good he felt. I unpinned my hair, letting it fall down my back. Tommy yanked my tracks, pulling me forward, and he pounded my pussy till I tapped out.

After three long, good, stimulating rounds of sex, Tommy and I lay on the floor entwined in each other's arms.

"Lana, I want to be able to trust you, but I'm not sure if I can." He ran his fingers through my tangled hair.

"If you give me the chance, I will show you that you can. I just want you to give me the chance. I know I can make it right." I leaned up, looking into his eyes.

"I want to tell you about the vision haunting me. The woman haunting me. I have to tell you about her if we are going to make it." He released a deep breath.

"This isn't a therapy session. This is two adults, friends becoming lovers, talking and healing. Just let it flow out naturally." I gave him a little smile to help ease the worry he might be having.

"My ex's name was Dareen. Well, at first, she told me it was Monica. She was supposed to be my girlfriend, but I found out I was just a pawn in a game for her to get my best friend Eric." He spoke as he pushed me off his chest so he could sit up.

"That's fucked up," I whispered.

"That's not the worst part. She was supposedly pregnant, but she said the pregnancy timeline lined up with her ex, Joe, who left her for Eric's wife's best friend, Jalisa. She had it out for all of them. She aborted the baby but told me it was a miscarriage. I wanted to give her all of me. I love her so much, I do. Even now, if she were still here, I would tell her how much I love her and try to save her from them. She didn't deserve what they did to her." Tommy disclosed all this information to me that I never knew about before.

I don't think that was all of Tommy's truth. He was still hiding something from me. "You said if she were here. Why did you say that? Did she move or something?"

Tommy's eyes wandered back and forth. His hesitation started making me suspect something fishy was in the air. "No, she died."

"I'm so sorry, Tommy. Do you want to tell me how?" I asked, praying he would tell me the details of my sister Dareen's death, which was truly Rebecca's.

"I found out she had siblings. She was from a set of triplets. Something is telling me she's still here with me. And maybe I found the wrong sister dead, but that's only wishful thinking, I assume." Tommy gathered his clothes and walked over into a corner to dress.

I was crawling on the floor toward him when I heard three gunshots ring in my office waiting area. Tommy motioned for both of us to hide until the gunfire ceased. Who would do anything crazy like that? Was it one of my clients? I did have a few suicidal ones, and maybe they were trying to give up on it all tonight. Curiosity kills the cat, and hopefully, I won't die in the process.

Tommy kept shaking his head, trying to keep me from looking, but I needed answers. I picked up my blouse and khaki pants from the floor, sliding them on as quietly as possible. Once I got dressed, I eased over by the door, cracking it open slowly. I got a glimpse of the shooter. I was in shock to see it was Dareen. Did she hear what Tommy told me? Who was I dealing with here? She's part of the reason Becca is dead. My mind couldn't wrap around all the craziness that I learned in such a short time.

I know I have to handle Dareen delicately. If not, who's to say she wouldn't try to kill me? Giving Tommy a slight smile, I worded "OK" to him before heading into my waiting room. Dareen was still shooting in the air. I just prayed that God would keep me covered and not let me get hit by a stray bullet.

As her finger was tightening around the trigger, I tapped her on the back to gain her attention.

"Sister. Darling sister, thanks for joining me." Dareen seemed bothered. Her eyes were bloodred, like she had been getting high or crying.

"What are you doing here? We need to get you out of here before someone sees you," I said, pushing her toward the unused stairwell to the left of the room.

"*No*. I want to talk. You got time to get dick but not talk to me? Is that part of the plan? Fuck him so he can be pussy whooped and is on our team? Or are you turning against me?" Dareen probed, yanking her arm from my grasp.

"Dareen, no one is turning against you. It's just us. If we don't stick together, we can't avenge Becca. I'm doing everything I can, and more, to get him to talk. But for him to leave, you have to hide. Once he's gone, we can talk, okay? I promise." I gave her a hug, then ran back to my office.

I waited for Dareen to disappear on the stairs before going back in. Tommy was fully dressed, holding a handgun. I was unsure what he needed that for.

"Tommy, put the gun away. Everything is fine. It was just one of my clients. I need to talk to them because they're having a suicidal moment. My job as their doctor is to make sure I keep them alive and rechannel that negative energy. Go home, and I'll call you as soon as I leave, okay?" I kissed him while groping his private area.

"If you say so. I'll call the police if you want once I leave," he offered, but Dareen didn't need the police or to be committed to a hospital. She needed love.

"No, it's okay. I got this, I promise. Just let me know when you get home. And maybe we can do round two later tonight or tomorrow."

"We can see. I'll try to free up my calendar," he teased as he grabbed a handful of my ass before leaving the office.

I watched him get on the elevator before looking for Dareen. When I went to the stairwell, she was gone. I hoped I didn't fuck up anything. Most importantly, I needed to outsmart her if she did have a hand in what happened to our sister. Tommy was genuine in everything he said. I could tell. But I needed to find Dareen quickly before anyone saw her, especially Tommy. I locked my office and ran through each floor looking for her, but she seemed to be gone.

Going into the parking garage, I heard more gunshots go off. I didn't know if it was Tommy or her who was shooting. Tommy's car sped right past me, and behind his tire tracks was my sister, lying on the ground, shot.

CHAPTER SIXTEEN

Dareen

The cement was so cold. This parking garage was getting blurrier and blurrier. Was I dying this time? Was Rebecca using Tommy to kill me because they thought she was me? Everything was becoming so dark.

I awoke on my bed, half-naked. I don't even remember how I got here. I tried sitting up in the bed, but the whole right side of my body was filled with pain. I looked at Lana as she came into the room, bandages and towels in hand.

"You're lucky it's just a flesh wound. I already got the bullet out," she said, cleaning off the blood around my abdomen.

"What happened? Who shot me?" I asked, trying to piece together the last few moments of my life up to this moment.

"Well, when I got down there, a car had sped off. Is there anyone who may want to hurt you?" Lana asked, while ringing out the rag soaked in my blood in a mixing bowl full of water.

"No . . . no one . . ." I stopped, and it came back to me. "Reneece. That ho. It *had* to be her."

"Okay, sis, listen to me." Lana tried to get me to relax while I fought her off me.

"Listen, dammit. We have to get you healed first. Then we can deal with her, if she's the one who did it."

"If she didn't, she had her punk-ass friend do it. I'm gonna kill them." When I tried to stand up, the pain hit me like a ton of bricks.

"Heal first. Kill last." Lana looked at me warmly as she wrapped the bandages around my waist.

"Hey, Laylani, thank you. I know you don't like that name anymore, but you taking care of me is more Laylani than Lana." I smiled back at her, feeling loved by my sister.

The night went on, and Lana checked on me several times. I was lying on the bed and checked the clock. It was eleven p.m., and I was hungry. I didn't see the light on in my sister's room. I'm sure she was asleep, and after the day she had, she deserved to sleep peacefully.

Taking my time, I slowly eased out of bed, one leg at a time. My right hand gripped the left side of my abdomen as a burning discomfort filled my body. I hobbled out of the room, but before I got to the kitchen, Lana appeared out of the bedroom, rushing to my side.

"Are you okay? Why are you out of bed?" she asked, helping me walk to the kitchen.

"I was hungry, and I needed something to eat. I didn't want to wake you." I grabbed hold of the brown bar stool by the kitchen counter.

"Well, let me cook you something." Lana went to the refrigerator and opened it. "Ummm, let's see. I have some chicken nuggets and stuff in the freezer, some eggs and shit . . . Maybe some breakfast foods?"

I giggled at my sister's attempt. "No, let's just go grab something or order out."

"We can't go out anywhere with you like that." She slapped her hands on the counter.

"But let's check out Grubhub. Let me grab my phone."

"Don't run, or you're going to fall," I shouted as I watched my sister scurry down the hall in her socks.

Lana tossed up her middle finger and disappeared into her bedroom. She reappeared a few moments later, sat beside me, and scrolled through her phone, going through the menus of the available restaurants. After searching through two pages, we agreed on Insomnia Cookies and ordered two dozen chocolate chip and peanut butter cookies. She sat up with me until about three a.m., eating cookies and watching reruns of *Martin*. We had so much fun together and ended up falling asleep in her bed, the TV playing in the background.

The following morning, Lana went off to work, leaving me in the house by myself. She was gone about an hour when my phone started buzzing from a text she sent. Thank goodness my phone was lying beside me in the bed.

Lana: Hey, sis. Just checking in. My first client just left. How are you feeling?

Me: I'm making it. I just woke up a few minutes ago.

Lana: Well, I arranged for someone to stay with you for the majority of the day. Just so I know you're eating and that you're safe.

Me: Well, who is it? You know we can't trust just anybody.

Lana: I promise I made sure you would be in good hands, okay? No worries.

Me: Okay, we'll see. But if they seem off, u better show up ASAP, client or not.

Lana: Well, I'm only a text or call away. I know u will be fine. (smiling emoji)

Me: Thanks, sis. I do love you, honestly. Thanks for everything u have done.

Lana: Anytime. I love you toooo.

An hour later, I was lying in silence, trying to collect my thoughts when I heard the door open. Whoever it was at the door didn't announce themselves. The person came into the room and stuck their head in, so I pretended to be asleep so they wouldn't bother me. I peeked my eyes open and saw that the person was a man. A nice, tall man. I thought to myself, Lana was trying to get me laid, having a man come in here to take care of me. As the male figure stood at the bedroom door, he made a call.

"Hey . . . Yeah, your sister is sleeping. Should I just wait for her to say something?" The voice sounded so familiar, I was trying to catch it.

"Yeah, I got you, Lana. I got this. You know Tommy got your back."

I was in shock. Did he just say *Tommy*? Did she *really* bring Tommy into this house? What the hell was she thinking? What part of the plan is this? Especially since I can't defend myself.

"Yeah, Doc, thanks for trusting me. First step in a healthy relationship. Go back to work. Maybe when you get home, if she's still asleep, we can have a 'private' session." When I peeked up again, Tommy was heading back toward the hallway.

I sat up slightly, trying to understand what was happening. My sister set me up, and when she got home, I would find out why.

Eric

My life was back in a world of turmoil. Reneece was on edge, and that's the last thing I needed with her being pregnant. It took us six months to push through the miscarriage she had with our last child. So, this was our second chance at expanding our family. Life is such a bitch, but Dareen was the devil itself. We were supposed to be past this psychotic-ass ho. I needed more answers about her family, and I intended to get them.

Since Tommy hit me up to let me know he was working from home today, I decided to do a little research before work. My first stop was the vital records office. Reneece called an old sorority line sister to give me access to the office before everyone showed up. I arrived there around six thirty in the morning. The brisk morning air chilled my bones just a tad as I ran into the back of the building.

Once inside, Reneece's friend Joan escorted me to the back of the office. She had already pulled out every piece of information she could find about Dareen and her family. There wasn't much there, and it frustrated me. I sat in the back room with ten envelopes containing nothing informative. I went over them several times until I got frustrated. It was close to opening time, and I had to disappear before anyone saw me. I gathered everything I could before heading out.

Once in my car, I drove to a local Starbucks to grab a coffee so I could go over the papers once again. I needed to open my mind so I could think clearly. We needed a trail to follow. We needed a way to dig deep into her history and see what we missed the first two times.

Dareen was alive. I felt it inside me. I never understood why she couldn't just let us be. With the time that had passed, surely she couldn't still be after me. What if it was one of the sisters who knew about her obsession and was toying with us? All these different scenarios went through my mind.

As I went through the third folder, I reviewed the birth certificates for her and her sisters. Her father's name was nowhere to be found on any of them, but their mother's name was Isabella Travis. The address provided for the mother was near Central. So, they grew up here. They know Durham better than anyone. I decided to stop by that address on my way to the office to see if anyone still lived there.

I arrived at the house, and it looked like no one had lived in it for years. The grass was tall, and the windowsills chipped and molded. It was like no one took care of the grounds. When I pulled into the driveway, I noticed a not-so-old green, four-door pickup truck in the backyard. Maybe if someone is here, they could help provide me with answers.

"Hello? Hello? Is anyone here?" I noticed the gates between my hood and the backyard were open. I pushed the steel gate back and walked through it.

"Sir, may I help you?" An older lady appeared out of the shadows near a wooden barn in the left corner of the yard.

"Umm, yes. I'm looking for the parents of Dareen Travis. See, I married her not too long ago, but she was battling depression, which I didn't know, and she killed herself last week. I thought that at least if her family didn't come to the wedding, they would come to her funeral." I pretended to break down in front of the woman, playing on her sympathy.

"You talkin' about my sister Isabella's daughter? The girls that our sister Mary raised?" She came a little closer to me, looking at me strangely.

"I didn't know she had sisters. She never told me anything about her family. Nothing, only they didn't want to come to the wedding." I sniffled, looking up at this woman who looked similar to Dareen.

"Come inside, my dear boy. You are family. You need to learn about your wife." This woman had to be in her late fifties. I looked at her closely, and she resembled Dareen, especially the eyes.

We went into the house, and the inside looked nothing like the exterior. Family photos covered the walls, a maple wood chest stood there with a pendulum clock, and anything I touched didn't have a speck of dust. And the wooden floors looked as if they were freshly mopped and waxed. The woman took me up some stairs and opened all three doors. She said that they belong to the girls.

"Let me show you Dareen's room. We kept the house like this, hoping she would come back and let us finish helping her." The woman went over to the wooden dresser with an oval mirror attached.

"Help her how?" I was curious about what she meant.

"See, our family on our mother's side has two things in common. We all birth triplets, and we all believe in our powers as a witch." She pulled out this book with a brown leather cover with a hole in it.

"I'm sorry, but did I hear you correctly? Witch?" I laughed out loud so hard I almost cried.

"Dareen and Rebecca embraced it the proper way, never for evil. Now, Laylani was different. She started using her voodoo and the magic we taught them to do horrible things when people picked on them or if she fought with her sisters." The woman passed the leather book to me.

"So, this book is . . . " I looked up at the woman, and suddenly, her back was turned to me, and she sobbed loudly.

"It's the book that we used to teach them spells and voodoo tricks. There's one in there to speak to the dead. Laylani cursed Dareen to make her unstable, and Laylani has a darkness in her that can't be overcome. We haven't seen the girls in years. Laylani comes in every once in a while to practice spells and use the voodoo dolls. She's the undercover dangerous one. She's like oleander. It's beautiful and polished, but poisonous and very deadly." The woman turned back around with a smile.

"Well, thank you for your time. Is it possible I could come back sometime? You can tell me more things about my wife and y'all's family," I asked, backing toward the door.

"Sure, Eric. I'll know how to find you. Let you know when it's a good time." The woman came closer to me. "Dareen talked about you so much before she disappeared. Even Laylani knew about you at one point. She would hide when her sister came in to talk or to get solace from this evil world. You take care now."

I nodded with a smile before heading out of that house as fast as possible. So, now, this shit just gets crazier. The triplets do voodoo, her sister Laylani was deadly evil, and Dareen was cursed? It was going to take some time to wrap my head around all of this, but first, I needed to head to work.

CHAPTER SEVENTEEN

Tommy

Damn, every time I fuck Lana, shit gets better and better. It was like she was in my head and into my deepest desires. Every sexual encounter turned into a different fantasy I wanted, except for a threesome. As we lay in her bed, I ran my fingers through her soft, wavy weave.

"I could lie like this is your arms forever," Lana said to me with a smile on her face.

"Yes, this is nice. What time is it?" I asked, looking down at her.

"It's ten o'clock. Do you have somewhere to be?" She sat up in my bed, turning to look at me.

"Outside of work, just you, my darling," I said, dragging myself out of bed in nothing but my socks.

"Well then, I guess I should be getting up too. I have a client coming in around twelve." Lana followed behind me into the bathroom.

Lana was fun, easy to talk to, and the sex was amazing. But something about her didn't feel complete. I know she wanted a relationship with me. But I wasn't ready to give her that part of me. Even Rayna didn't get that out of me, but I tried. It's just that I still wanted my Dareen back. I used Lana as a distraction, but Dareen was what I really wanted and needed.

I stepped into the shower. The water temperature wasn't too hot, and it wasn't too cold. I grabbed my bottle of Old Spice body wash and lathered it over my body. I was washing my balls when Lana joined me in the shower.

"Daddy, what's wrong?" she whispered in my ear while running her fingers down my spine.

"Nothing, darling. Just trying to clear my mind before work." I felt her grab my dick with one hand and caress my balls with the other.

"There's nothing you should worry about. I'm all you need, Tommy." She kneeled in the tub. "Say it, Tommy, I'm all you need."

I didn't know what had gotten into her, but the way she was sucking my dick at that moment was all I could think of. The way she moaned with my dick in her mouth turned me on so much. Lana sucked me dry, giving me one of the best orgasms off of head I ever had. Finally, she got off her knees and smiled at me wickedly.

"Why you looking like that?" I asked, going back to washing my body.

"Because you and your soul now belong to me." Lana slowly exited the tub, going back into my bedroom.

I thought she had crazy tendencies, but she was worth dealing with them. By the time I finished my shower and got dressed, it was almost eleven thirty. Lana was two steps ahead of me. While we said our goodbyes, I agreed to stop by and peek in on her sister before going to the office. Interestingly, she hadn't told me her name.

On my way to Lana's house, I received a call from Eric just as I turned my phone off silent. I answered the call through the car's Bluetooth.

"Yo? I know I'm running late, fam, but I'll be at the office in a minute," I informed him, hoping I didn't miss anything important.

"Tommy, there's some information I found out today. I'm calling an emergency family meeting at my house after work. This shit is crazy, man." Eric sounded unlike himself, as if he were spooked.

"E, man, what the hell is going on? You sound like you losing your shit, bro." I wondered what caused him to seem so dismayed.

"Tommy, I don't think anyone would see this shit coming. But we have a meeting at two with some new clients. So, I'll see you soon." He disconnected the call.

I was really worried about my friend. Someone or something spooked the shit out of him. It was evident in his voice. Before arriving at work, I stopped at a McDonald's to grab a bite to eat. Luckily, I beat the lunch crowd, so I was able to order and get my food pretty quickly.

I arrived at work, and Eric was just arriving. He signaled for me to follow him. I was nervous, considering our brief conversation earlier. I wasn't sure what was on his mind.

"Tommy, close the door," he instructed as he went over to his wooden chest in his office.

"What's going on, bro? You ready for the meeting?" I leaned on the wall next to his diploma from NCCU.

"Tommy, we are up against some shit I don't think we're ready for. I went through files on Dareen and her family. There was an old address there that my gut told me to check out. The house looked abandoned from the outside, but I went inside, and the house was so beautiful." He went on and on about this house.

"Okay, so, what did you find in the house? Wait, how did you get in? Did you break in? You know you can get arrested for that." Verbalizing the obvious, I just prayed Eric wasn't that stupid.

"Hell no. Thanks for stating the obvious. But no, to answer your question. This older lady came out from behind the barn they had and escorted me into the house." Eric pulled out a bottle of E&J and a crystal shot glass and asked me, "You want a shot?"

"Yeah, sure, pour me one. I ate something other than pussy this morning," I joked, trying to lighten the mood.

"Here." Eric passed me the glass. "I gotta show you something." He kneeled, grabbing his all-black briefcase from under his desk.

"The lady gave me this." He slid a brown notebook across his desk in my direction.

"What's this?" I opened the book, and it seemed filled with weird poems and recipes.

"It's some type of voodoo or magic shit Dareen and her sisters used to do. There's one that still practices, and she supposedly cursed Dareen. Get this. Every female in their family has triplets at some point. So, luckily, we dodged a bullet with Dareen terminating that pregnancy." Eric reclined his chair back, taking another shot of the liquor.

"So, you're telling me that Dareen was cursed and that all three of them practiced voodoo?" This sounded crazy to me. I couldn't help but laugh—not at Eric's expense—but it seemed like someone was toying with us.

"What if she's telling the truth? The woman knew my fucking name and shit. A fucking stranger knew *my* name and knew about me and Dareen. So, excuse me if I'm starting to sound a tad bit crazy, but something is strange, and maybe this is it." Eric got up from his chair and moved toward his window.

"Aye, listen, man. I may be crazy and working through some shit. But you ain't crazy. Give me the address, and I'll check it out after we meet up with everyone tonight. Let's see if I get the same information as you." I placed my shot glass on the table. "We have a meeting to prep for."

We met with one of the city's popular real estate agents, Carl Trumanee, and his wife, Portia. They recently purchased a cottage-style house on the outskirts of Raleigh and wanted us to remodel it from top to bottom. With an $80,000 check for any upfront costs, who could say no?

After all the paperwork and contracts were signed and reviewed, we went back to the office to close up for the day. Reneece reached out to Eric to let him know that Joe and Jalisa had arrived at the house. I wanted to meet with everyone, but I knew the adrenaline in the room would be crazy. Taking a different route since Eric had given me the address of Dareen's childhood home, I headed there to get some answers of my own.

The sun was setting, and the temperature was dropping just a tad. After all, it was fall. I arrived at the home Eric described and noticed one dim light peeking through the window. I parked my car across the street, then headed to the front door. I knocked and knocked, but no one answered. Finally, after my fifth attempt, a woman came to the door.

"Yes, may I help you?" The woman seemed older but not elderly. She opened the door in her purple housecoat with matching slippers, and a head full of rollers.

I flashed her a smile and said, "Yes, ma'am. I'm sorry to disturb you. My friend wanted me to come by here for him. See if you could tell me more about Dareen's sisters. His name is—"

"Eric. I met that handsome young man earlier today. You are Tommy." She looked me up and down like she was sizing me up.

"Yes, ma'am, my name is Tommy," I responded with a subtle wince.

"Well, come on in. I don't bite now. You know, my Laylani mentioned you to me once on the phone." The woman let me into the house, then locked the door behind me.

"I'm sorry, I don't know Laylani. Is that a friend of Dareen's or Eric's?" I questioned, trying to figure out what was going on.

"You're funny. Laylani said you had a playful, warming spirit. I can feel it. But Laylani never told you she was Dareen's sister. She came out first, then Rebecca, and lastly, Dareen. She said y'all been dating for a year and you still didn't know?" She wobbled into the kitchen while mumbling to herself.

I was waiting for her to come back when I felt something, or someone, hit me from behind. I was hit so hard that it knocked me out. I had no clue how long I was out, but I awoke in a soft bed wrapped in a navy-blue blanket. I jumped out of bed and rushed to the door when Lana appeared.

"Baby, where are you going?" Lana stood in the middle of the hallway with a mixing bowl in her hand.

"Lana, where did you come from? How did I get here? What the hell is going on?" I stood back, unsure of what transpired.

"Tommy, I found you stumbling down a street. I was making a house visit to one of my younger clients because their mom called me. I was leaving their home, saw you, and damn near dragged you inside the car. I brought you here since my house seemed closer." Lana was moving in on me, and honestly, I felt trapped.

My palms were sweaty, and my heart fluttered. I was looking around when someone appeared in the shadows, mouthing the word "Run." I searched my pockets, but my phone, wallet, and keys were missing.

"Tommy, don't make this hard. Lie down and rest. I told you I'm taking care of you. I got you, I promise." Lana inched her way toward me, coming closer and closer.

"Lana, give me my things, and I'll come back tomorrow, or when I get home, you can come over." Reaching out my hand, I hoped she would return my property to me.

" *No.* You will go lie down while I cook our dinner. This is not a suggestion. *This is an order,*" she screamed at me.

This wasn't like her. Lana didn't seem crazy or possessive before. I knew I had to play my cards carefully if I was going to make it out of this house. I lay in her bed, not making a sound or moving. Then it hit me. What if Lana was really Dareen in disguise? Am I 'bout to die?

CHAPTER EIGHTEEN

Dareen

I couldn't believe what I heard from my bedroom door. Laylani had finally shown her face. I was wondering when my *real* sister would show up. She thought I had forgotten who she truly was. It doesn't matter if you change your appearance, your body, hair, or eye color. Who you truly are will eventually come out. Tommy thought I was bad, but Laylani is ten times worse than I am. She craved the love our father never gave. Our father was very abusive, and it took that one last beating that made our mother introduce us to the voodoo world.

We were taught to use it for positive things. No matter what my father did, my mother protected him even when she shouldn't have. We never knew that Laylani was practicing on voodoo dolls until one day I caught her with it. She cursed me after I told Momma on her. Until today, I never believed I was cursed, or that it worked, or that we had magic in us. If that were the case, I would've had Eric to myself. I wouldn't be here two fucking years later.

Honestly, I felt sorry for Tommy. Out of those three men, he was the one who cared for me the most, and he always had pure intentions. Just too bad that we couldn't have been more. It wouldn't be fair for me to attach myself to him when Eric and I were still in love with each other. Tommy didn't deserve to be tortured anymore, but he was going to help me.

Lana was walking down the hall toward my bedroom with a plate of food. I hobbled back into my bed and lay there like I had no clue what was occurring in the rest of the house. She knocked on the door twice before entering.

"Hey, sis, are you hungry? I made dinner for us. So, sit up, and let's find a movie and enjoy our meal." I wasn't sure if I had Lana or Laylani in the room with me at this point.

"Thanks. What did you cook?" I asked her, sitting up in bed and pulling my rolling bedside table toward me.

"Cajun chicken stew and rice. Just like Momma used to make. It was definitely worth being in the grocery store early this morning. Why don't you go ahead and taste it?" She started eating and smiled at me.

"So, I have a question," I said, mixing my rice with the stew.

"What's up, sis?" Lana looked up at me sideways as traces of the stew dripped from her bottom lip.

"Is Laylani in front of me or Lana?" I stopped eating, looking directly into her eyes.

She stopped eating and took a napkin to clean the excess food from her lips. Waiting to see which version of my sister I was about to get an answer from made me nervous. Lana, I could handle, but Laylani would kill me before I got the chance to kill her first.

"I'll tell you what's up if you tell me what happened to Rebecca. Tommy told me that it was you who caused the bullshit. They wanted you, *not* Becca. You killed her, didn't you? *Didn't* you?"

My sister snatched my plate from me and threw it against the wall.

"*I* didn't kill Becca. Yeah, they wanted me 'cause I was fighting for a man who was supposed to love me. But he *always* chose that bitch Reneece over me. Rebecca looks just like us. Well, me, since you changed yourself. We were beautiful. They took her, thinking she was me. I watched each of them, from Eric, Reneece, Jalisa, Joe, and your precious Tommy, mutilate and murder our sister. When I got there, it was too late," I screamed as I propped myself up on the bed. The day I watched my sister die at their hands, I was stuck in a state of shock, trying to understand why they hated her. I didn't know why they would want to hurt, let alone kill, her. I wanted to help her, but my body just wouldn't move. I blamed myself for it every day.

"My name is Laylani, and I will punish *you and* all of them for your crimes against my sister. How fucking *dare* you play with me like this. You forgot who I am? Mommy was weak by not teaching you the dark side of our world. All of us would still be together if you had just embraced what was inside you." Laylani was out to play, and I knew to beat her, I needed to match the darkness.

"Laylani, there are some to punish, but Tommy isn't one of them. I know you have him. He's the only one who mourned me and loved me. If you care for him, you must let him go." I came to Tommy's defense because it was only the right thing to do.

I realized this was my Karma coming back on me. Maybe there are some things I should've done differently, but I wasn't going to let Laylani win this. She tackled me on the bed, gripping my neck tightly. I clawed at her hands, but she wouldn't let up. The more I struggled, the tighter her grasp.

"I'm going to make you pay. You *hear* me? I *hate* you. You could've been my partner. This didn't have to be your path. You had to wake me up, and now, I see I was needed more than ever. Where's your other half? Why aren't you talking to her, huh? I will *kill* you." Laylani tossed my head back and forth into the bed, keeping her tight grip on my neck until everything went black.

Lana

I left Dareen's still body on the bed. I strangled her enough to knock her out for a while. Between her and Tommy, they just wouldn't let me be Lana. They woke my inner demon, who sought blood from anyone and anything that fucked us over. I tried so hard to love Tommy. And yet, here we are with him snooping around our family home. What wasn't brought to light should've stayed hidden.

I made Tommy a bowl of the stew, adding a special touch. In it was a mixture of herbs that my grandmother used to make for us to help us sleep. I added a root of valerian and kava. With both of them together, it would knock Tommy out for a while. I was in love with this man, and I don't think he could see it, but I planned on helping him find his way.

I walked into my bedroom. Tommy was lying in my bed, flicking through the channels. Standing in front of the television, I placed the plate of food on the stand, then turned to face him.

"Are you hungry, my love? I made us a nice dinner. If you want, I can feed it to you." I took off my shirt, revealing my purple silk bra.

"Nah, I'm not hungry, and you can put your shirt back on. I'm not really in the mood to fuck right now." Tommy jumped out of bed and grabbed his shoes from beside the headboard.

"Why are you doing that? Where are you going?" He couldn't leave me. He belonged at our home, and he was going to stay, even if I had to make him.

"Lana, I really think I should just go home. I have a lot of work to do. We have a new client, and I have blueprints to work on. I'll call you when I'm done, OK?" Tommy gave me a peck on the cheek and walked out of my room.

I promised Tommy I would take care of him. I wanted to do that, but I realized part of taking care of him was still allowing him to make decisions and letting his emotions be heard and validated. I checked in on Dareen. She was still knocked out cold. I quickly grabbed my black hoodie, tights, and black rain boots. I needed to make a trip to visit his business partner and see why my sister had to risk it all for him.

Eric was listed as Tommy's emergency contact. So, I made it my business to keep that number in my phone just for situations like this. I left the house and went straight to my office. When I got there, I sent Eric a text message. I knew it was late, but I figured his wife wouldn't mind him leaving for business.

Me: Hello, Eric. I'm Dr. Lana Morane, Tommy's therapist. I just met with him, and I'm worried about him. Do you mind meeting me briefly in about thirty minutes? I want to talk to you and see how we can get together to help him out.

Eric: Yes, anything to help him. What's the address?

Me: Perfect. I'll send it and see you then.

I knew it would take me that exact time to travel back and forth to Tommy's house. I set up some recorders in my office so I could record everything that happened. While I waited for Eric, I took a quick trip to Tommy's house. I was sitting in my car, blasting "Posed to Be in Love," by Kevin Gates. I am going to have Tommy not just as my friend, but as my husband.

Tommy's car was missing. He was supposed to come straight home. That motherfucker lied to me. Where could he have gone? Lucky for me, I had my key to his house made the last time he spent the night. I let myself in to see if there was any sign of foul play in our relationship.

Inside his bedroom, I went into the closet. Using the flashlight on my phone, I searched through some of the boxes he never opens when I'm around. Old receipts were in one of the boxes. The next box was an old Nike shoe box. I grabbed it from the bottom corner of the closet. The box contained a ring and pictures of Dareen. I was confused. I thought we were over this. Obviously, he wouldn't move on till I got rid of her for good.

I really didn't want to kill Dareen. I just needed her to think so. But now, I have no choice. I hate competition, and I won't be losing to someone like her. She isn't even half the woman I am. I didn't understand how he could still love her since he said she did him so badly. Suddenly, I heard someone enter the house just as I received a text from Eric saying he was on the way.

I waited in the corner of the closet, hoping not to be caught. Tommy came into his bedroom and stripped at the bathroom door. When I heard the shower turn on, I took that as my chance to escape.

I made it out of Tommy's house without being seen. I arrived at my office, and Eric was already in the parking lot. He followed me to the building and to my office. Once finally inside, I sat beside him on the sofa.

"So, Doc, what's going on with Tommy?" Eric was very handsome. I see why my sister was so hooked on him.

"Well, Tommy and I had a breakthrough earlier today. He told me the image haunting him was of a woman named Dareen. I was wondering if you could help me know more about her or why she would be haunting him." I sat Indian style beside him, wondering if he would tell me the truth.

"Well, Dareen messed Tommy up. From what I know, he loved her, but she broke his heart. I just know she disappeared. Tommy really didn't say much," Eric said, lying to me.

He had one chance to make the right decision and tell me the truth. I licked my lips as I thought of what to do next. I hopped on top of him and grabbed my letter opener, which I use as a decoration, from the small table beside me.

"See, you're wrong. You and your buddies killed my sister. You thought it was Dareen, but it was our sister Rebecca. *I* am the one you should've been preparing for. Dareen is a saint compared to me and what *I'm* capable of." I jammed the letter opener into the side of his leg.

"You crazy bitch!" Eric pushed me off of him, making me hit my head on the coffee table.

"Oh, Eric, you aren't going home. I hope you told your wife goodbye and made love to her for the last time before coming here." I reached under the cushion of my chaise, grabbed my .45 caliber, and fired away.

Eric fell to the ground after the second shot. I walked over to him. "This is for Rebecca and for torturing her." Then I shot Eric in his stomach and walked away, leaving him there to bleed to death on my carpet: one down and four to go. I was going to make sure Dareen was the last to go, and Tommy was going to help me.

CHAPTER NINETEEN

Eric

I lay on the office floor of the woman who was supposed to be Tommy's therapist, bleeding from the gunshot wounds. All I could think of was my family. I wouldn't get to see my two children grow up, and my wife would have to handle everything by herself. Who was going to take care of Reneece when I was gone? A tear fell out of my eyes as I tried to get my phone out of my pocket. I was lying there when I noticed the door pushing back open. She was coming to finish me off if I wasn't dead yet, I thought to myself.

"Listen, I'm going to get you out of here," a man whispered through the shadows.

"I'm not going to make it anywhere. Let me die here," I moaned, already given up on life.

"Reneece didn't hire me to watch you all for no reason. I'm Jackson, and I'm going to make sure you make it back to your wife." He pulled me off the floor and helped me to the parking garage.

"What now?" I mumbled after coughing.

"I'm taking you to my homie to take care of the wounds, and you'll recover there until you can go home." Jackson put me up in the backseat before getting in on the driver's side.

Thirty minutes later, we were at a hospital. He took me through an emergency exit and carried me into a secured operating room. A man was already waiting for us, dressed in scrubs. I received a shot in my arm, and seconds later, I was out.

When I awoke, I was in a hospital bed, and Reneece was right on my side. I was so happy just to see her face again. She was my world, and I couldn't imagine leaving this life without being able to hold her one last time.

"Am I in heaven?" I asked, cracking a smile at her.

"No, but as long as we have each other, it's our heaven on earth. I love you so much." Reneece took my hand and rubbed it against her cheek.

"You won't believe who did this to me." I licked my dry lips and shook my head in disbelief.

"You said you were meeting Tommy's therapist. So, was Dareen there? Like, I don't understand how this could have happened." Reneece pulled her chair closer to mine.

"No, it wasn't her. It was her other sister. She said we killed their sister Rebecca, not Dareen. So Dareen is alive, but she may be the only one who can lead us to her." I gave my wife the lead that we needed. We didn't just have one problem. Now, we have *two*.

"So, you're telling me Tommy's therapist is also that psycho's sister? And out of the three of them, we killed the wrong one? Eric, this is unbelievable. Is this the fucking Twilight Zone? I'm going to handle this while you get it together." Reneece's face tensed up, and her anger flushed her face.

"No, I can't risk anything happening to you all. I can't physically keep my three babies safe, so you tell Tommy and Joe about the situation. I trust them to do the right thing." I fought back my tears as I looked at my pregnant wife, knowing I failed to protect her and our family.

"Eric, we will not sit here and wallow in self-pity. You will be fine, and I will make it my business to make sure everyone who hurts us pays. I will be careful, but this has to stop." Reneece stood up, leaned over the bed, and kissed my lips.

"I love you so much," I whispered to her.

"I love you too, babe." Reneece walked out of the hospital room, leaving Jackson at the door, guarding me.

"Sir, I'll be here throughout the night until your wife returns. If you need any food or anything, I will test it first to make sure there's no poison in it." Jackson made me aware of his current duties.

"And my wife put you up to this? How did she find you?" I wondered where this man came from.

"She contacted me a few weeks ago and told me someone was trying to harm you all. But she wasn't sure who it was. I've been following you and your friends since then." Jackson grabbed one of the visitor chairs and sat down.

"Well, I'm lucky my wife is always ten steps ahead. I would've died if you didn't show up. So, thanks, fam," I said before I raised my hospital bed.

"I hope to only be so lucky in a few months. My girlfriend and I got engaged two weeks ago. We set a date yesterday. Here, you wanna see a picture?" Jackson came over and showed me his camera roll, full of pictures of him and his fiancée.

"Just know if she's worth the proposal, she's worth the universe. When you remember that, y'all be able to get through anything." I gave him some advice as I thought back on Reneece's and my relationship.

As the time passed, I prayed that everything was going smoothly. I was praying for their safety when the pain meds finally started to kick in, putting me straight to sleep.

Tommy

After that weird encounter with Lana, I went home to wash the day off of me before heading to Eric's house. By the time I showered and dried off, Reneece shot me a text, informing me that my best friend had been shot. We automatically knew it was either Dareen or Lana. They would be the only people out for him, potentially hurting all of us.

I took off on my way to the hospital when Reneece called me, telling me to come to their house instead. Switching lanes, I changed directions, doing at least ninety on the highway. The one thing I could do right now is protect Eric's family. When I got to their home, Jalisa and Joe were arriving as well. We greeted one another before walking to the doorstep.

Reneece let us all in, and then we made our way into the living room. By now, it was about 11:30 p.m., and Reneece broke down the situation to us.

"Eric is stable but still in the hospital. We don't have just one but two problems on our hands now." Reneece took a seat, rubbing her pregnant belly.

"Tommy, your therapist was the one who shot Eric, not Dareen. When she left him there for dead, she told him her sister was Dareen and not the other woman we killed. We need you to find her so she can lead us to Dareen. Then we can kill them both." Reneece's hands clenched the arms of her recliner.

"Wait a minute. Are you sure? That sounds a little far-fetched. I couldn't see her doing anything like that." I don't know what was going on here. My mind drifted back to earlier. I needed my own answers without them prying.

"Well, you didn't think Dareen was like that either, and look what happened. You're not the best at judging character, Tommy. Especially if you been fucking them," Jalisa spat out, sitting on the floor near Reneece's legs.

"Aye, I don't have shit to do with someone else's actions. You think if I knew she was related to Dareen that I would be going to see her to deal with my issues?" I shouted at her, feeling a whirlwind of emotions hit my body.

"Watch how you talk to my wife, okay? I told you that before, rude boy. Fuckin' pussy wad, I'll kill you." Joe shoved me in my chest, coming to the defense of his rude-ass wife.

"You know what? Y'all deal with this shit yourselves. Y'all blame me for Dareen. Now, you blaming me and my therapist for what happened to Eric? Watch your backs because from now on, I'm watching my own." I grabbed my jacket and stormed out of the house.

I couldn't believe my so-called family was acting this way toward me. How am I supposed to know if someone is after us if they show no signs of it? How the fuck was I supposed to know that Lana was Dareen's other sister? I couldn't know because I went to her for help. I hope they can band together without Eric to get shit done. But me, I have different plans in mind. My first stop on ending this crazy cycle is Lana's house.

CHAPTER TWENTY

Dareen

I finally awoke from a deep sleep, and my sister was gone. For the first time in a long time, I was afraid. I feared my sister all over again. Laylani has always been a deep-rooted evil bitch that I couldn't stand to be around at times. But she was also very protective and never let anyone hurt us. It felt like my time was coming to an end. Like I could die at any moment. There was only one thing I wanted to make right if my gut feeling was to come true. I needed to apologize to Tommy. The last thing I remembered was him being told to head to Lana's bedroom.

If Laylani were in front of him at that moment, she might have knocked him out too. I had to get my strength up so I could check out the house and possibly fight my sister. I used my portable food table tray as my crutch, slowly making my way out of the room toward Lana's master bedroom. Walking as quietly as possible, I peeked into the bedroom, but no one was there.

I looked into the mirror that hung from the bedroom door, and my reflection just shook her head.

"*You can't save Tommy. We need to save ourselves and deal with Laylani later. We have no plan, and we're injured. This looks like a losing battle. Think smart, Dareen. We can't go into this blindly.*" My reflection had a point. There's no way to beat Laylani without figuring out her plans.

"We should go to Tommy. If I can get enough energy to drive, we can go to Tommy's house. He'll protect us. He still loves me. Then we use that time to come up with a way to get Laylani away from all of us," I told myself before leaving the bedroom.

Making my way toward the front door, I suddenly heard someone outside. *I hope that's not her,* I thought. I saw a pair of Nike slippers in the corner by the kitchen counter, so I slid them on just as the front door opened. I had no time to get anything to protect myself. I was standing in the dimly lit kitchen when Tommy appeared in front of me.

"Tommy?" I whispered, making sure I wasn't seeing things.

"Dareen? Dareen, is that you?" Tommy came closer to the kitchen, locking eyes with me.

"Yeah, it's me, Tommy. How are you?" I asked in a soft, caring tone.

"How am I? You *can't* be serious. I was going crazy wishing I could have saved you, and *here* you are. Why are you here?" Tommy stopped at the brown leather bar stool adjacent to me.

"Tommy, we can talk about that later. First, I need you to go before my sister gets back. She's *not* who you think she is." I was trying to warn him that he didn't deserve any more pain.

"*No*. You're going to answer me. Tell me what the fuck is going on and why you're here." Tommy punched the marble countertop with his fist as he angrily spoke to me. "Dareen, you are going to tell me *everything*. And if I feel like it's the truth, I *may* help you this time. But you have to tell me *everything*."

"Lana, your therapist, is my sister. She changed her name and appearance so she wouldn't look like me or our other sister, Rebecca. The way you all killed Becca placed an anger in my spirit, not just for losing her that way when she begged for mercy, but to know that's what would have been done to me. I wanted revenge for her. So I found Lana and told her what I needed to so that she would be on my side. I never thought our plan would turn out like this." I tried to give him a brief summary without all the details, but it wasn't good enough.

Tommy placed his phone and keys on the counter just as Lana appeared behind him. It was like God knew it was about to go down. I could hear the thunder roaring outside as my sister was standing there with her gun in hand. I moved my focus to Tommy. He was still looking at me with his big ole brown eyes. I murmured, "Duck." Instead of doing what I said, he just sat there looking like a deer caught in headlights.

"Tommy, you just couldn't let her go. If it's not your horrible friends, it's *her* you keep running to. What about *me?* What about *our* love? I'm going to have to kill her myself just for us to be happy." Lana raised her gun at me and cocked it.

"Laylani, stop it! Come on, we can find a different way. You can have Tommy. Killing me is going to do *what,* sis? Come on, let's *think*. Be smart." I ducked down behind the counter, trying to escape the shots.

"You are *crazy*. You gonna be buried right next to your beloved Eric. I already took care of him. Neither of you deserved his loyalty. I am going to enjoy killing each and every one of you." Laylani moved closer to the kitchen counter, and a shot went off in the air.

I peeked up, and Tommy had Laylani by the waist, trying to get the gun out of her hand. My abdomen was hurting so badly, but I needed to help him. I stood up and reached over to the stove, where a pan sat there. Pan in hand, I swung it, hitting her across her face. My sister seemed unbothered by the hit. Head butting Tommy in the chin, Laylani was able to get free from his grasp.

"Sister, tsk-tsk. You know better. I am Laylani. Remember who the fuck I am. And when you get to hell. tell them *I* sent you there." Laylani charged at me like a bull.

Falling backward on the floor, my sister climbed on top of me, punching me. Blow after blow into my kidneys and wound. I grabbed her head, banging it into the wall. She leaned up, rubbing her head, which gave me time to move away. As I got farther down the hall, she grabbed my ankles, dragging me toward the living room.

"*Stop* it, Lana. Come on. This is crazy." Tommy tried pulling her off me, but every time, she just came right back.

"No, that's *not* my name. My name is Laylani. I tried to make you fall in love with me. First, I did it the natural way, and then I tried love spells. Nothing worked. You still had her pictures in your closet. *Her*. The woman who you said made your life hell a year ago. She's alive, so what, fuck me then? No love for *me?*" Laylani turned around, slapping Tommy in the face as she sobbed.

"You're jealous that he loves *me?* You want to kill *me* because he loves me? You killed Eric for what? Eric did nothing to you." I used her wooden nightstand to help balance me as I stood up.

"No, Eric's not dead. He barely made it. Lana or Laylani, we were just fucking. We *never* were in love. I couldn't love you if my heart belonged to another. What we had was nice. It's only been a few months, and you're acting like we been together for years. You *ain't* my girl. I'm not pressed 'bout you. So, you wanna take out some shit? Take it out on me then. But killing my best friend *isn't* going to make me love or want you." Tommy was taunting her, and Laylani was falling for it.

"No, you don't mean that. You *can't* mean that. I'm your world. You're *my* world. I tricked her dumb ass into killing that Rayna bitch. And if you just let me kill her, we'll be okay. Tommy, tell me you love me. Please. just *tell* me." Laylani grabbed Tommy's face, kissing him, trying to make a point, I guess.

While my sister was distracted by the kiss, I noticed her gun on the floor. It was my chance to switch the tables and be in control, knowing I wasn't going to kill her unless I had to. I just needed her to be scared and bend to my will. I was just about to grab the pistol . . . when the kiss was broken, and she caught me.

"Oh no, sister, what are you doing?" Laylani tried reaching for my legs again, but Tommy grabbed her, trying to hold her.

She struggled in his arms as I grabbed the gun off the floor. Coming toward her, I aimed the gun at her, and she just smiled at me.

"If you got the guts, kill me, sister. Kill me like they killed Becca. How you let them kill Becca . . . You gonna shoot me? Shoot me then, bitch." My sister screamed for me to shoot her, but I couldn't.

"Tommy, let her go." I placed the gun on top of the coffee table in her living room. "Laylani, I'm not going to kill you. I never would kill you or Becca. I love y'all regardless of everything that's happened in our family over the years."

Tommy released his hold and backed up toward the kitchen, where his phone was still on the countertop. My sister and I stood between the coffee table and the kitchen, staring at each other.

Laylani looked at me with a smile. "You're right. I do love you. Well, at one point in my life, I did."

She immediately grabbed the gun, cocked it, and fired four rounds at me. I fell back toward the TV stand as she came closer to me. If she didn't kill me with the first few shots, she was going to finish me off now. Tommy came rushing into the living room, and seeing my body on the floor, he ran up to Laylani, and with the barrel of the gun at his chest, she fired her last three shots into him. We both lay on the floor, and I cried for him. I didn't want him to die. My body was getting colder by the second. I took one last look at the world around me and heard, "I love you," before death snatched my soul.

CHAPTER TWENTY-ONE

Lana

Finally, after all that scuffle, my sister's body lay still on my living room floor. I went over, kneeling beside her, feeling for a pulse, but none was there. What had I done? I shouldn't have taken things this far. I could've helped her, but she wouldn't just stay away. If she stayed away, I wouldn't be like this. I lay next to her lifeless body, crying out for a miracle to bring her back to me.

With all we learned as children about different remedies and spells, there was nothing for death. I wanted both my sisters back, but it was too late. I curled up into a fetal position so I could sleep beside my sister one last time.

It was 6:30 a.m. when I heard a noise inside the house. I looked around, but I couldn't see anything because it was still dark. Not knowing what was happening, I made my way into the hallway to see one of the bathroom lights on. Creeping down the hallway, I shouted hello to see if anyone would respond.

I pulled open the bathroom door, but no one was there. I turned off the light and headed to my bedroom when someone suddenly snatched me up.

"Thank goodness I invested in a bulletproof vest, huh? We're going for a ride," Tommy said, covering my mouth with a towel and dragging me out of my home.

He shoved me into the back of a black kidnapper van, as we called it back in the day. As soon as I got inside, someone hit me on the head and knocked me clean out.

I woke up in what looked to be an old warehouse. Around me stood three other people and Tommy. I sat in a wooden chair, my feet and hands bound by rope.

"What the hell do you think you're doing? Tommy, Tommy, untie me right now," I demanded as I scrutinized the people in the room.

"Nah. Tommy's not going to do anything. Actually, all of this was Tommy's idea. Only difference between you and your crazy-ass sister is he doesn't care what the fuck we do to you." A pregnant lady appeared with a baseball bat in her hands.

"And who the hell are you?" I asked, holding my head up high.

"The man you tried to kill yesterday was my husband. One thing you and your sister have in common is that y'all both have issues with loving the wrong men or men that don't belong to you." The woman swung the bat at my ribs.

"We should make this quick. Soon, people will be up, and there are less things we can get away with," Tommy said, sitting in the corner, smoking a cigarette.

"Tommy, *please,* tell her to stop this," I begged as she repeatedly hit me with the bat.

"You're asking the wrong motherfucker for mercy. You should ask *me,* ugly bitch," the woman screamed before she spat in my face.

"You disgusting bitch! You all will die! Just wait till I get free. I'll kill *you* first, fat bitch," I shouted back, trying to shake the spit off my face.

"Bitch, I ain't fat. I'm pregnant. Something *you'll* never get to be." The woman walked away from me, tossing the bat on the ground.

"So, what? You're going to kill me? How do you think you can kill me without going to jail? A respected therapist and someone involved in her community, with no record? Y'all have no proof of me doing anything. I'll die but be in heaven watching each of you rot in jail." I laughed, knowing they probably wouldn't do anything more than beat me.

"There's always ways around things like this." A dread head came from beside Tommy with a machete in his hand.

"Maybe she's right. If Tommy was right, she had already killed the one we needed and wanted dead. So, do we *really* need to kill her?" The other woman in her jean romper stood in front of the man with the machete, blocking him from coming any closer to me.

"No loose ends. She dies too. We don't need her tryin'a pop up and pull some shit like her sister. This ends today," the pregnant woman yelled back at the woman.

No one said another word and allowed the dread-headed man to walk toward me.

Tommy

Just like that, it was over. It was all over. Joe took one big swing at Lana's neck and cleanly chopped off her head. There was no need to prolong her death. She didn't deserve any torture. Honestly, we all just wanted to move on with life, and for good this time.

I looked down at the concrete floor of the same warehouse where we killed her sister Rebecca and saw Lana's head on the ground. I threw up immediately after seeing that. I don't do well with decapitation or anything of that nature. I honestly thought he was just going to stab her or something.

"Now, what are we going to do?" I asked after I threw up one more time.

"We wrap up the head in the plastic wrap. We'll leave the body here till night, and I'll come back and finish her up," Joe replied as he took a bottle of ammonia to clean off his blade.

"Well, I'm sure Eric will be glad to know we were able to handle this without him. No fatalities, and more importantly, no more Dareen." Reneece walked out of the warehouse with a smile on her face.

As everyone else rejoiced in Dareen's death, I was back to being heartbroken. When they dropped me off down the street from Lana's place, I called 911 as I approached the house. I told them there appeared to be a break-in at my girlfriend's home. I was advised not to go in, but I told them I wanted to see if she was okay.

I went to the back of the house, where Joe met me to break down the back door. We put on gloves and quickly trashed the place before the police arrived. Joe ran out the back as the sirens approached. I gave him my gloves and kneeled beside Dareen's cold, dead body.

"I'm sorry I couldn't save you. But thank you for trying to save me. You had good in you, and I knew it all along. I'll love you always." The police came in, telling me to back away from her body.

The coroners took her body while I was giving my statement to the police. All of my friends received their happy ending, but me. I felt like my life was over and that I would never find true love.

EPILOGUE

Tommy

Two years had passed, and life was finally moving forward for me. Eric had made a full recovery. Reneece was able to give birth to a set of twins, a boy named after Eric and a girl they named Aiko. Jalisa and Joe finally made it down the aisle. I was even one of the groomsmen after Joe and I settled our differences.

I threw myself into work at first, trying not to deal with my emotions. I went back to therapy, but not without doing a background check first. My new therapist was a male, which made it so much easier not to go back down the path of mixing business with pleasure. Working with him, I faced my demons and realized that Dareen was my blessing in disguise. I never knew how to love a woman before her. In the midst of my coming out of my darkness, a new light unexpectedly walked in one day.

I was at the office when this beautiful, dark chocolate woman walked in with an older couple. Eric had just stepped out for lunch, and I was working on a blueprint for a new restaurant.

"Hello, we are the Jonans. We were supposed to be meeting with Tommy and Eric today around two, but we are a little early," the older woman with salt-and-pepper hair said to the receptionist at the front desk.

“Hey, I’m Tommy. You all can follow me. Eric should be in shortly.” I greeted each of them with a handshake before escorting them to the back.

“This is our daughter, Brisa. She will be the main one overseeing our business. I hope you both get to know each other. She’s great at everything she does,” Mrs. Jonan said to me.

I was enthralled by Brisa’s beauty at first sight. After many months of business meetings, I finally got the courage to ask her out. Brisa had the cutest smile, and her natural curly hair was so soft. She gave me a peace I hadn’t felt ever. I think I finally found the one for me.

On Valentine’s Day, I set up a romantic picnic at the Durham Bulls ball park. It cost me a pretty penny to rent it out for the night. I had her meet me there around eight in the middle of the field.

“Tommy, this is so beautiful,” Brisa said, clinging to my arm.

“Just like you.” I guided her to our purple blanket that lay on the grass.

I lit two candlesticks, set up a picnic basket filled with her favorite sweets, and poured a bottle of Apple Cîroc, which was also her favorite.

We ate everything in the entire basket and danced under the moonlight to Beyoncé’s song “1+1.”As we danced, I looked into her beautiful, almond-shaped, hazel-blue eyes and knew this was what real love felt like.

She sat down after a couple of songs, and we finished off the last of the goodies. Then I reached into the wooden basket and pulled out a little black box with a red ribbon tied to the top.

“Here, I got you a little present.” I passed her the box, waiting for Brisa to open it.

“Wait, babe, is this . . .” She looked down at the beautiful 14k white gold diamond engagement ring with a 3-carat diamond in the middle.

"Yes. Yes, Brisa, I want to spend the rest of my life with you. I loved before, but I never loved anyone as I love you. You give me such peace and joy, something that I've never had in my life. All I want is to spend the rest of my life with you. So, I ask you, will you marry me?" I slipped the ring on her finger as I awaited her response.

"Let me think about it . . . Of course, I will. But first, here." Brisa passed me a white envelope.

Inside the envelope was a sonogram and a pregnancy test. "I'm going to be a father?"

"Yeah, I found out this morning. I couldn't wait to tell you." Brisa smiled with a twinkle in her eye.

I had never been more aroused than I was at that moment. I climbed on top of her and made passionate love to her in the middle of the field. I finally received my happily-ever-after. I now knew what true love and happiness were, and I was ready to embrace them wholeheartedly.

The End

Thank You

I want to thank all of my readers, new and old, for all their support over the years. You all have been such a staple in my career, and I can't thank you all enough.

Special thanks to Racquel Willaims, T'ann Marie, and all my pen sisters who have kept my head above water and constantly encourage me.

Most importantly, to my nieces and my children, I love you all.

To my sister, Tonya, I hope I'm making you proud as you look down on me from heaven.

Love Always

Kandie Marie